THE CHOSEN ONE

"Lay your hands on his head!" Linda commanded, thrusting the limp heap of flesh toward him. Luke's face was already covered in frothy black blisters. "Do it!"

What if I fail? What if—

Holding his breath, Harold reached out with his right hand and placed the tips of his fingers on the top of Luke's greasy scalp.

The bubbling ceased.

The barn froze.

If anyone was breathing, Harold didn't hear it. Not a sound. His eyes roved over Luke's body—very meticulously, inch by inch. He felt as if he were examining a single frame of film on a long reel. As far as he could tell, the plague was caught in a state of suspended animation. Luke wasn't melting. The blisters remained; blood dripped from open sores . . . but he was alive. He was solid. He was *whole*.

My greatest miracle.

"You did it," Luke gasped. A shaky smile spread across his cracked lips. "You *did* it!"

Harold's heart broke into a savage, hammering thump. For a moment he thought he might faint.

My greatest miracle.

"The Chosen One," Linda whispered.

About the Author

Daniel Parker is the author of over twenty books for children and young adults. He lives in New York City with his wife, a dog, and a psychotic cat named Bootsie. He is a Leo. When he isn't writing, he is tirelessly traveling the world on a doomed mission to achieve rock-and-roll stardom. As of this date, his musical credits include the composition of bluegrass sound-track numbers for the film *The Grave* (starring a bloated Anthony Michael Hall) and a brief stint performing live rap music to baffled Filipino audiences in Hong Kong. Mr. Parker once worked in a cheese shop. He was fired.

COUNT DOWN

JUNE

by
Daniel Parker

Simon & Schuster
www.SimonSays.com/countdown/

First Aladdin Paperbacks edition May 1999

 Produced by 17th Street Productions,
a division of Daniel Weiss Associates, Inc.
33 West 17th Street, New York, NY 10011

Cover design by Mike Rivilis

Aladdin Paperbacks
An imprint of Simon & Schuster
Children's Publishing Division
1230 Avenue of the Americas
New York, NY 10020

Library of Congress Cataloging-in-Publication Data
Parker, Daniel, 1970-
June / by Daniel Parker. — 1st Aladdin Paperbacks ed.
p.   cm. — (Countdown ; 6)
Summary: In a world where turning twenty-one seems to mean certain death by a horrible Plague, the forces of the demon Lilith and the Visionaries who believe in the Chosen One continue to be drawn west toward a final confrontation.
ISBN 0-689-81824-6 (pbk.)
[1. Supernatural—Fiction.] I. Title.
II. Series: Parker, Daniel, 1970-   Countdown ; 6.
PZ7.P2243Ju   1999
[Fic]—dc21

To Liz Craft

The Ancient Scroll
of the Scribes:

In the sixth lunar cycle,
During the months of
Sivan and Tammuz in the year 5759,
The Chosen One will rise from
the depths of her own woe,
Gathering inner strength.
Freed from false hopes,
with a need to wreak vengeance upon her enemies.
And the earth shall again bask in a fleeting glow.
The Demon requires a burnt offering:
A mass sacrifice of righteous
souls to feed her powers,
To match the strength of the Chosen One,
Drawing both the Traitor and the
False Prophet into a web of deceit.
The two shall serve
unwittingly the Demon's needs,
Becoming her most valued servants.
The False Prophet will
perform his greatest miracles.
And even the Seers will believe him.

Strong floods wait by a blue bath
and poke seeds at the seas.
The whale eats eggs and drops teeth.
Six twenty-one ninety-nine.

The countdown has started . . .

The long sleep is over.

For three thousand years I have patiently watched and waited. The Prophecies foretold the day when the sun would reach out and touch the earth—when my slumber would end, when my ancient weapon would breathe, when my dormant glory would blaze once more upon the planet and its people.

That day has arrived.

But there can be no triumph without a battle. Every civilization tells the same story. Good requires evil; redemption requires sin. The legends are as varied as are the civilizations that spawned them— yet each contains that same nugget of truth.

So I am not alone. The Chosen One awaits me. The flare opened the inner eyes of the Visionaries, those who can join the Chosen One to prevent my reign. But in order for them to defeat me, they must first make sense of their visions.

For you see, every vision is a piece of a puzzle, a puzzle that will eventually form a picture . . . a picture that I will shatter into a billion pieces and reshape in the image of my choosing.

I am prepared. My servants knew of this day. They made the necessary preparations to confuse the Visionaries—all in anticipation of that glorious time when the countdown ends and my ancient weapon ushers in the New Era.

My servants unleashed the plague that reduced the earth's population to a scattered horde of frightened adolescents. None of these children know how or why their elders and youngers perished.

And that was only the beginning.

My servants have descended upon the chaos. They will subvert the Prophecies in order to convert the masses into unknowing slaves. They will hunt down the Visionaries, one by one, until all are dead. They will eliminate the descendants of the Scribes so that none of the Visionaries will learn of the scroll. The hidden codes shall remain hidden. Terrible calamities and natural disasters will wreak havoc upon the earth. Even the Chosen One will be helpless against me.

I *will* triumph.

PART 1

June 1, 1999

New York City
7:30 A.M.

When Sarah Levy stood very still and faced due north, she could almost convince herself that everything was fine.

She had to concentrate hard, of course. She had to ignore the memory of the past two days, ignore the twinges of panic and horror that shot through her empty stomach. She couldn't look behind her, either. She had to stare straight ahead. But if she did all that, if she *focused*—she could just barely manage to forget what had happened.

Couldn't she?

New York City is normal, she repeated to herself.

Yes. Yesterday she'd stood for several hours in the exact same spot—right at the halfway point of the Verrazano Bridge, right where the slim arc of the highway peaked over the water . . . and the view was just how she always remembered it. This was home.

Nothing had changed. The Statue of Liberty rose over the harbor a few miles away, squat and green in the rising sun. Across the mouth of the Hudson River, the twin towers of the World Trade Center stabbed up into the sky like two giant, upside-down silver fangs. Spread below her was the jagged cityscape of

5

Brooklyn. She might as well be staring at a giant, life-size poster of her old hometown. It *looked* like paradise, didn't it?

There were no fires, no ruins. Nothing was falling apart. Even the leaves on the trees were dazzlingly bright, shimmering in the morning breeze. It was the height of the late spring bloom. The whole city seemed poised to wake up from a good night's sleep, as if the air would soon be filled with the roar of traffic and honking horns and shouting voices. Only there were no people at all.

This isn't the way it's supposed to be when the world ends.

Hadn't her dead brother said something like that? She thought he had . . . back in Israel on the second day of the New Year, the day after the melting plague struck, swiftly and inexplicably turning every single adult and child around them into a puddle of black slime. Yes. Josh had looked at the blue sky and the deserted highways and empty towns and wondered why the hell everything still looked the *same*.

But New York was supposed to be different. America was supposed to be different. It was supposed to be untouched, teeming with people of all ages, going about their business as if nothing had ever happened. . . .

Still, there was one problem with the picture. One single clue that a devastating calamity had occurred here as well. The grasshoppers. They were everywhere. Luckily they seemed to be dying off—but their bodies kept falling in a continuous drizzle, hitting the water and the bridge with a spotty *pat, pat, pat*.

A few of them struck Sarah's head. She frowned and swatted at them.

Go away, she thought. Her glazed eyes narrowed behind her glasses. *Stop ruining it—*

She wasn't alone. Somebody was standing beside her on the bridge. She glimpsed a shock of long red hair out of the corner of her eye.

"Hi, Aviva," she murmured.

"Um—um . . . Sarah?" Aviva stammered hoarsely.

Sarah smiled. "Isn't the view amazing?" she asked.

"Sarah, are you all right?"

All right? Sarah's smile faltered. "Why?"

"Don't . . . I mean, don't you think we should be going?" Aviva choked out.

No, Sarah *didn't* think they should be going. Couldn't Aviva see that she was trying to enjoy a moment of peace? Just one single second? Was that too much to ask? If Sarah thought they should be going, they would have already gone.

"I just don't understand why we're hanging around here," Aviva added in a shaky voice. "Is there a reason why you aren't—"

"Where do *you* want to go?" Sarah demanded. She kept her gaze pinned to the Statue of Liberty. "Where?"

"I—I—I think we should go west."

"Why?" Sarah snapped. She knew she shouldn't be getting angry. Now was *not* the time to start a fight. But she couldn't help herself. Every time she'd been forced to think about reality in the past two days, a wild fury reared up inside her. "What's out west, anyway?"

7

Aviva hesitated. "I was hoping *you* would know," she said softly after a moment.

Finally Sarah whirled to face her. "Me? How?"

"Because you're the . . ." Aviva left the answer hanging. Her blue eyes flitted around the bridge, over the smashed trucks and twisted car wrecks that now filled Sarah's field of vision. "Because I'm *what?*" Sarah yelled. Her voice cracked. "Because I'm the Chosen One? Well, you know what? I quit. How's that? How's . . ." A lump lodged itself in her throat. Her eyes fogged—and then, much to her surprise, she was sagging into Aviva's arms and bawling like an infant.

"No, no, don't cry," Aviva whispered desperately. She ran a trembling hand through Sarah's tangled, shoulder-length brown hair. "Please, Sarah. Don't worry. We'll be all right. We'll figure it out. Just don't . . . just relax."

Okay, okay. Sarah straightened and sniffed, then took off her glasses and rubbed her eyes. *Get a grip.* She wasn't going crazy, was she? No. She would stop. No more lunatic denials of the truth. No more fits of hysteria. Her parents were dead; the city was dead; Ibrahim, the boy she loved, was dead. Despite everything she'd been led to believe these past two months, America was no different than any other place on the planet. It was just one of a million disaster zones. And she simply had to accept those facts. Period.

"Are you sure you're okay?" Aviva asked again.

Sarah nodded several times. "Fine," she croaked, putting her glasses back on. She craned her neck and peered toward the Brooklyn shore. A lone white exhaust tower jutted from the choppy water, sticking up at a skewed angle. It was all that remained of the sunken hulk of *The Majestic* . . . the cruise ship that had been Sarah's home for the past two months. She sighed deeply. "Where's everybody else?"

Aviva bit her lip and lowered her gaze.

"What is it?" Sarah asked.

"They're all gone." Aviva lifted her head. "I'm the only one left."

Sarah blinked. *What?* For a moment she thought she misheard. Her brain was too muddled. There was no way—

"They decided last night, Sarah," Aviva continued tremblingly. "When you were asleep. They blamed you for the shipwreck, I guess. I mean, you were the one who wanted to come to New York so badly. And then when we got here, and the grasshoppers attacked us and we crashed and everything—well, I guess they thought you were fooling us all along." Her lips began quivering. "You kept telling us America was going to be a paradise."

Good God. Sarah gulped. She had no idea what to say. She had truly believed that America *would* be a paradise. What about the rumors? What about the radio she'd heard on the ship, those signals that came from New York? She and Ibrahim had listened to those same stupid commercials over and over again. Why were commercials being broadcast if the city was no longer functioning? It wasn't her fault. Those commercials had lured her here and she'd come running— like a dog on the scent of a phony cookout. . . .

But in the end, it didn't matter. Nothing mattered except the fact that hundreds of kids had either drowned in the shipwreck or vaporized or bolted. And now Sarah was all alone.

"What should we do?" Aviva whimpered.

Sarah just shook her head.

Aviva began pacing rapidly back and forth, her brow tightly knit. "What about the scroll? Don't you think we should try to get the scroll?"

"How?" Sarah mumbled. Her eyes wandered back to the shore. "It's trapped at the bottom of the ship."

"Can you scuba dive?" Aviva asked, glancing up at her.

Sarah shook her head.

"Neither can I," Aviva muttered. She began pacing again. "But maybe we can, I don't know—maybe we can teach ourselves how. I bet we can find a sporting goods store somewhere that sells scuba gear—"

"Forget it, Aviva," Sarah interrupted. "Anyway, the scroll has been underwater for two whole days. I'm sure it's ruined."

"No, it's not!" Aviva shouted. "It *can't* be ruined. You saw when it was shot. Remember? The bullet holes closed right up. And when they tried to burn it, it wouldn't burn. It's magic, Sarah. *You* know that!"

Sarah swallowed. That was true, she supposed. Her granduncle's ancient parchment had mysterious powers . . . powers that she couldn't even begin to understand.

But *she* didn't have powers. None that she knew of, anyway. She might be the Chosen One, but it hardly mattered. She could still suffer. She could still experience pain. She could still be wrong and selfish and misguided. No, she was just a person, like everyone else. And if she were stupid enough to try to teach herself how to scuba dive, she would die. It was that simple. The scroll was gone—forever out of their reach. Without its prophecies to guide her, there was no point in even trying to *be* the Chosen One. It didn't mean a damn thing anymore. She hadn't even known what it meant in the first place.

"How come you still believe in me, Aviva?" she found herself asking.

"Because of what you *showed* me," Aviva whispered. "Because the scroll is three thousand years old, and it talks about *your* life. I was the only one on that boat who could actually read it, remember? And you told me that your granduncle had it hidden away in a special place in his house in Jerusalem because he knew it was the only thing that could stop the Demon. He knew it was the only thing that could save us. *All* of us."

Sarah didn't reply. Had she really said that? Maybe she had. But at this point, that conversation seemed very, very far away—as if it involved somebody else in another place at another time. And in the face of all the loss and death and destruction, it hardly seemed to matter.

"But that's not even the real reason I still believe in you," Aviva went on. For a moment she looked as if she were about to cry. Her voice was strained. "I believe in you because I saw you in a vision. All of us did—all the Visionaries. And all of us feel the pull out west. *Something* is going to happen out there.

Something big. And when we get there, hopefully you can figure it out."

"Hopefully," Sarah whispered. But the word was empty.

"So will you go west with me?" Aviva asked.

Sarah shrugged. Why not? It wasn't as if she had any reason to stick around New York. Besides, what did she have to lose? She'd already lost everything: the scroll, her parents, her brother, Ibrahim. She began to trudge back across the bridge—and at that moment she caught a glimpse of something she hadn't noticed before. Written across the Brooklyn-Queens Expressway, in painted orange letters thirty feet tall, was this:

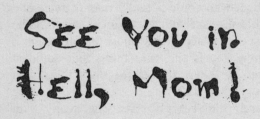

"I wonder what kind of creep went through all the trouble to do *that*," Aviva muttered.

Sarah sighed. "Not a creep. Somebody smart. Somebody who figured out that there isn't any hope at all. For any of us."

TWO

187 Puget Drive,
Babylon, Washington
11:45 A.M.

Things to Do Today

1. Wake up. (Okay, not necessarily.)
2. Consume rousing breakfast of three beers.
3. Trick Caleb into taking off at least some of his clothes.
4. Think of some way to pay Leslie back for everything. Has to be good. Has to be more than good. Has to blow her mind from here to Pluto. (Note to self: Must not involve booze.)
5. Pass out and start over.

Ariel Collins leaned back in the sofa and gave her diary a satisfied nod. Amazing. She'd already accomplished *three* of the five tasks she'd assigned herself for the day—and it wasn't even noon. Her father would have been proud. There was something truly admirable in managing to get bombed before lunchtime. Yup. Dad always knew she was a go-getter.

Unfortunately, however, there still remained the issue of task number four.

It was so damn *frustrating*. Her lips curled in a frown. What could she possibly do? She'd been driving herself crazy over this all week. The problem was that nothing—absolutely nothing—could measure up to what Leslie had done for her. Zilch. Not unless Ariel saved Leslie's life, rescued her from the clutches of a psycho (a psycho *sibling*, no less), hooked her up with the boy of her dreams, and then brought her back to her own home.

Oh, yeah . . . and only if Ariel managed to do all that in one week.

Ha! She had a better chance of reuniting the five original Spice Girls. And they were all dead.

Well, Ariel *wasn't* going to quit. No way. She was just getting started. The crisp morning buzz fired up her brain. Now she understood what people meant when they talked about "creative juices." They were talking about beer. *Get those creative juices flowing.* No wonder every rock star, writer, and artist was a drunk. Booze was inspirational. It cleared the dull grays from the mind and cast each thought in a rosy Technicolor glow. Of course, Ariel usually forgot any brilliant ideas after a few sips. But that was why she had the notebook.

On the other hand, she wouldn't mind at all if a *few* things slipped her mind. . . .

Especially Brian Landau.

She winced. She'd been thinking about her ex-boyfriend way too much. He was still trapped inside the Washington Institute of Technology, still locked in a classroom in Trevor's private little prison. How did he even *get* there? The worst was that there wasn't a damn thing she could do about it. She couldn't get within a hundred yards of WIT without getting shot at—

"Ariel?" The front door rattled. "Ariel? Anybody home?"

She glanced up from her notebook. The living room spun for a moment. *Man.* She must be a little more plowed than she thought. "Leslie?"

"Yeah. Can I come in?"

"Sure." Ariel closed her diary and tossed it onto the coffee table, narrowly missing the row of empty beer bottles. *All right.* Time to forget about Brian. Time to forget, period. Maybe she should have another cold brew. . . .

The door flew open, and Leslie strode right in—dressed, as usual, like an off-duty stripper. She was wearing a tight black miniskirt and a tank top. A ratty knapsack was slung over her shoulder. She closed the door and glanced at the coffee table, then smiled at Ariel. "I hope those are bottles of apple juice," she stated in a dry voice.

Ariel grinned.

"Got one of those for me?" Leslie asked nonchalantly.

"Whoa, whoa . . . wait a second." Ariel's eyes widened. "Am I hearing things? Leslie 'I'm-a-health-freak' Tisch actually wants a *beer?*"

"That's Leslie Arliss Irma Tisch to you, baby." She

paused. "On second thought, you're right. A beer would probably make me barf. I'm just bored."

"Me too. Sit down. We can be bored together." Ariel chuckled to herself. She used to hate the way Leslie called people "baby." But now she realized what the real problem was. It wasn't the way Leslie spoke, or the way she dressed, or the way she acted. No. Ariel had disliked Leslie for one simple reason: because Leslie was gorgeous.

The sad truth was that she made Ariel look like drab city—and Ariel had always been at least *semi*confident in her own looks. But dull brownish blond hair couldn't compare to Leslie's wild dark curls. Neither could Ariel's eyes. Hers were watery hazel; Leslie's were a striking black. Plus there was the fact that Ariel could pass for an albino if she stood next to the girl. Leslie always looked as if she'd just gotten back from the beach. And as for their respective bodies—well, *that* was just plain depressing.

"So what are you doing in here, anyway?" Leslie asked, tossing her knapsack onto the floor. It landed with a heavy thud. She slumped down in the old, battered easy chair. "Besides getting drunk, that is."

Ariel shrugged. "Trying to think of a way to pay you back," she said simply.

"Come on." Leslie groaned. "You don't have to—"

"I'm serious." Ariel tried vainly to summon an earnest expression but ended up giggling. "At this point, I'm too wasted to lie."

"Uh-oh," Leslie mumbled. "Is this gonna be like a Bud Light commercial? Are you gonna get all weepy and say, 'I *love* you, man'?"

Ariel smirked. "I just might. I haven't had a lot of practice with stuff like this. See, it's, like . . . well, it's complicated. First of all, I've been a total bitch to you. And you saved my life. Twice, actually. Then you got me together with Caleb. Then you—"

"I *didn't* get you together with Caleb, Ariel," Leslie protested. "All I did was—"

"No, no, let me finish. You *did* get us together because you told me how he felt. Okay, I know that sounds cheesy. But you backed off from him. You—"

"That was nothing!" Leslie cried, laughing. "I shouldn't have fooled around with him in the first place. It was stupid. He *loves* you. It's not even—"

"Just shut up and listen," Ariel insisted, but she was laughing now, too. "Okay? Look at it from my point of view. A week ago my own brother had me locked up and starving to death. My own goddamn *brother*. I thought Caleb was dead. Now I'm back in my own house, sleeping in my own bed, partying every night . . . and—and . . ."

"Getting to know Caleb in the biblical sense?" Leslie suggested wryly.

"Something like that." Ariel reached forward and lifted an empty beer bottle. "But the point is, *you* broke me out of WIT. You made it possible. You hooked me up with Caleb. So here's to you . . . *baby.*"

Leslie sighed and shook her head. "Wow. I'm speechless. Where is Caleb, anyway?"

"In bed." Ariel smiled. "He went back to sleep. It's been a rough morning."

"Tell me about it." Leslie moaned.

Ariel raised her eyebrows. "What do you mean?"

17

"All the fighting." Leslie peered at her questioningly. "Isn't it driving you crazy?"

"The fighting? What are you talking about?"

Leslie blinked. Then she laughed again. "Um, Ariel? When was the last time you went outside?"

"I . . ." Ariel's face reddened. She put the bottle back down. When was the last time? Yesterday? She couldn't even remember. *Jeez.* That was pathetic. She was probably due for a breath of fresh air. At the very least, she should open the curtains.

"You *are* aware that, like, hundreds of kids are partying on your front lawn. Aren't you?"

Ariel nodded uncertainly. Hundreds? Her eyes wandered over to the drawn shades. She did know that some people were hanging out in front of the house: the dregs of the Seattle survivors, some random kids, some Chosen One weirdos. But she didn't know there were so many. Of course, Leslie might be exaggerating. Still, it was a little disconcerting to think that she'd been so wrapped up with Caleb that she'd missed a huge raging party . . . in her own yard.

She strained her ears. There were voices outside. Lots of them. It seemed as if the volume was rising, too.

"Anyway, the Chosen One freaks are totally harshing on everyone else," Leslie went on. "It's the drinking. They're really uptight about it." She grinned ruefully. "Needless to say, the guys who *are* drinking aren't thrilled. Nobody's thrown a punch or anything yet . . . but you know how boys can be."

Ariel scowled. A fight? This was no good. These

kids were on *her* block. In a way, she was their host. Well, not really—but still, breaking up a fight was as good an excuse as any to leave the house. Summoning her strength, she forced herself out of the couch. It wasn't easy. She felt as if an invisible string connected her butt to the cushions. She teetered for a moment as blood drained from her head.

"Easy, there!" Leslie teased. "You all right?"

Ariel nodded. "Yeah, yeah," she finally managed. "Let's go check it out."

Leslie pursed her lips. "You sure? You might get hit with a flying bottle."

"I'll duck." Ariel marched to the front door and yanked it open.

Damn. She frowned, squinting out across the yard. The street had definitely seen better days. It looked like an environmentalist's worst nightmare, littered with garbage and beer cans and thousands of dead locusts. A bunch of kids were gathered in a semicircle around two guys at the curb. The guys stood face-to-face, only inches apart. Clearly they weren't chatting about old times. A few idiots were egging them on.

"Come on, Rob—take that mother out!"

"He's a wimp, man! Whatcha waiting for?"

"Swing, dude!"

Leslie appeared at Ariel's side. "See what I mean?" she muttered.

Ariel grunted. It was ridiculous. Why did ninety-eight percent of the male population always have to act like gorillas? Without even thinking, she stormed across the lawn.

"What the hell is going on out here?" she demanded.

The crowd fell silent. The boys glanced at her. Both looked annoyed.

"Any particular reason you have to do this in front of *my* house?" she barked.

One of the boys stepped forward. "This has nothing to do with you," he stated in a tightly controlled voice. "It has to do with the Chosen One. The Chosen One wants for them—"

"How do *you* know what the Chosen One wants?" Ariel interrupted. "Did you talk to him on the Psychic Party Hot Line?" A few kids laughed.

The boy's face darkened. "That's not funny."

Ariel rolled her eyes. "Look, I don't mean to be rude, but I don't see the Chosen One around here. If you want to believe in him, fine. But if other people want to enjoy themselves, what's the big deal? You aren't gonna win any popularity contests trying to act like a cop."

He didn't say anything.

She glanced at the other guy. "And if drinking bums out Mr. Chosen One here so much, just don't do it in front of him, all right? Go down the block. You can walk, can't you?"

The guy frowned. But he kept his mouth shut, too. He looked a little shocked, in fact. So did everyone else. Ariel folded her arms across her chest. In spite of her confident glower, she was pretty shocked herself. Where had all *that* come from? Maybe it was the liquid breakfast talking. But apparently the diatribe worked. There were some disappointed grumblings, some dirty looks, but the crowd began to break up.

20

"Nice job," Leslie whispered in her ear.

Ariel shrugged. It was funny. She actually felt like kind of a badass.

"You know, there are a lot of people out here," Leslie said after a moment.

"Yeah?" Ariel cast her a sidelong glance. "So?"

The faint beginnings of a smile appeared on Leslie's lips. "If we could actually get these dopes to go along, we'd make a hell of a posse. We could round up some baseball bats and rush WIT once and for all. Trevor wouldn't stand a chance."

Rush WIT? Ariel swallowed. A fleeting memory flashed through her brain—dim and disjointed, but undeniably nauseating . . . a pastiche of blood and dead kids and Trevor's leering face. The face that was like an evil mirror image of her own. And it was all bound up in *guilt*. She'd been responsible for something terrible.

"I don't know," she said. "I think we should just stay away."

Leslie sighed, then lifted her shoulders noncommittally. "Maybe. But think about it. Every single kid out here has one thing in common. They all hate Trevor's guts. He locks up anyone who talks about the Chosen One. He tries to *kill* everyone else. And he still has all the electricity and most of the food in this town. I mean, he can actually watch TV. It's like nothing ever happened to him. Why can't *we* live like that? It pisses me off. I *know* it pisses you off."

Ariel gritted her teeth. Leslie was right. It did piss her off. Why should Trevor go on living like some kind of mad scientist—when all he did was torture people? For all she knew, Brian was in there right now, getting beaten or starved or worse. . . .

"All I'm saying is that we should try to get people together," Leslie murmured. "Because we all want to get what Trevor has. Every single one of us. Especially you."

CHAPTER THREE

After wandering aimlessly for hours, Sarah was beginning to think that she and Aviva were the only people alive in the entire city. Either that or she was dreaming. The deserted streets had a surreal, almost nightmarish quality—wholly familiar and utterly alien at the same time.

On the surface, the vast urban sprawl really hadn't changed *that* much. There were still the rows of crumbling brownstones, the nondescript warehouses and grocery stores, the seedy bars and housing projects. The only stark difference between *then* and *now* was that everything was covered in a layer of dead grasshoppers. Their tiny carcasses shifted endlessly in the wind, like fallen leaves.

There were other, lesser differences, of course. The cars weren't moving. The traffic lights were blank. The near total silence was a little disturbing, too. And occasionally Sarah would see *something* . . . some uncertain evidence that bizarre and dramatic events had taken place. A few blocks had been looted—littered with broken glass and burned debris. One had been completely cleared of cars. Another was blocked off

23

by an enormous, reeking mound of black-stained clothing. It was probably fifty feet tall.

And everywhere—*everywhere*—were the same spray-painted messages: on the walls, on the billboards, on the cars and houses and storefronts. Death to the Pigs. Death to the USA. Lies, Lies, Lies. The Plague Is Our Only Salvation.

So where *was* everybody?

At exactly four P.M. a church bell rang. It shattered the still air, reverberating off the empty buildings: *gong . . . gong . . . gong . . .* Sarah remained petrified for the entire time—even after it stopped. For some reason, the ringing terrified her. It just didn't *belong.* It was like a lonely ghost, crying out of the past, begging for everyone to come back.

On and on Sarah and Aviva walked, mile after mile. The sun inched across the sky. Shadows grew longer. But Sarah didn't rest. No. In spite of her exhaustion, in spite of her hunger and shinsplints, she refused to even slow down. She just wanted to get out of Brooklyn. As fast as possible. The absence of people, the repetitive shuffle of footsteps, the stillness . . . all of it was starting to crack through the thin veneer of her sanity. She could sense something bad, a palpable tension in the atmosphere—as if a storm were just about to break.

But the sky was a cloudless blue.

I'm not going crazy, she reminded herself. *I'm not going crazy. I'm not going . . .*

*　　*　　*

"Flatbush Avenue!" Sarah suddenly cried. It seemed to jump out of nowhere—a broad street sign suspended over the dead traffic lights. She grinned. It was like the promise of water in a desert. "This turns into the Manhattan Bridge," she jabbered, unable to contain her relief. "We can take this straight into Manhattan and then cross the George Washington Bridge to New Jersey and then keep going west. . . ."

A burst of energy sent her running down the street. She skidded around the corner to the left and jerked to a stop.

My God!

The Manhattan Bridge was swarming with people.

She gasped, blinking. She couldn't believe it. There must have been hundreds of them up there; thousands, even. It was incredible: a miniature city, a carnival. Dozens of huts and tents and plain white flags poked out from the swirling mob. She could also see a few buses and trucks . . . they had been completely transformed, painted with bright colors and stacked with homemade additions: towers, decks, even a pyramid. Wisps of smoke rose into the sky. The distant roar of voices floated past her on the wind.

"Wow!" Aviva cried, running to catch up. "What do you think it is?"

Sarah shook her head. A jittery, nervous excitement seized her. The bridge was close. Closer than she expected, in fact. The entrance was only two long blocks away, marked by one of the familiar steel suspension towers. She took a step forward, then paused.

25

Wait a second. Her eyes narrowed. In the glare of the afternoon sun she could see the dark silhouettes of a group of boys heading toward her.

"Hey!" one of them called. "Oh, my . . . I don't believe it. Is that *Sarah?*"

Sarah's joints seem to freeze. *I know that voice.* She shielded her eyes from the sun with her hand. A tall, handsome African American boy was leading the group.

"Hey!" he called again. He broke into a jog. A tentative grin spread across his face. "Sarah? Sarah *Levy?*"

Sarah's jaw dropped. *Oh, my God.* She *did* know this guy. She'd gone to high school with him . . . Darrell Ewing. He was president of the student body. They weren't exactly friends, but she knew him. *Everybody* knew him. He was kind of hard to miss. For one thing, he looked like a model. He also made a big production of hanging out with as many different cliques as possible—even Sarah's lowly little circle of straight-A types. *Look! Aren't I a great guy? I even like nerds!* She had a feeling he never listened to a single word she said. He was just showing off his perfect smile until someone else came along.

"It *is* you!" he cried.

The next thing Sarah knew, Darrell was sweeping her up in his arms, squeezing her so tightly, she could hardly breathe. She couldn't even squeeze back. She was too bewildered. One moment she was convinced she'd never see another living soul—the next she was getting a bear hug from an old classmate.

"I don't believe it," he repeated, shaking his head

and laughing. He stepped apart from her. "Sarah Levy. How are you?"

She stared at him, openmouthed. *How am I?* She had no idea how to answer that. How was *anyone?* How was *he?* He didn't look as picture-perfect as he once had. His face was drawn—as if he'd aged ten years in the past six months. The scheming politician's sparkle was gone. Then again, she supposed that *she* looked a lot older, too.

"Are you okay?" he asked, suddenly sounding concerned. He shot a quick glance at Aviva. "I mean, are you sick or hungry or anything?"

"I'm a . . . uh, little tired," Sarah finally managed. She glanced at the other boys. They all stood behind Darrell, eyeing her with the same worried looks.

"Uh . . . Sarah?" Aviva murmured.

"I'm—I'm sorry," Sarah stammered. "Darrell, this is . . . Aviva." She swallowed. She was going to say "my friend Aviva." But was Aviva really a friend? Or was she more of a *follower*—some poor, lost kid who foolishly clung to the delusion that Sarah could somehow save her? The truth was that Sarah hardly even knew Aviva. They were two strangers who had been thrown together, completely at random.

"Come on, Sarah," Darrell murmured gently. He took her arm and began leading her toward the bridge. "We can deal with the questions and introductions later. I'll show you a place where you and your friend can take a nap—"

"Sarah?" Aviva interrupted again. Her eyes darted among the boys. "I mean, no offense, but I don't know . . . I don't know if this is such a great idea."

She paused, struggling to smile politely. "Don't you think we should be going? You know, west?"

Sarah hesitated. *Not really,* she thought. She was too tired. She was too tired to even think. Besides, what was the point of going west right now? She'd just found somebody she knew, a *friend.* Well, almost a friend. And she'd found a group of kids who by all appearances were healthy and relatively happy. What were the chances of *that?* No, at this moment she didn't care about following visions, or about being the Chosen One—or about *anything,* in fact. At this moment she simply wanted to let fate lead her wherever it might lead her. And if it led her to a place where she could sleep and forget and *escape* . . . well, so much the better.

"We'll talk about it later," Sarah whispered. Before Aviva could utter a word of protest, she leaned against Darrell and allowed him to escort her toward the bright, sun-dappled steel of the Manhattan Bridge.

FOUR

WIT Campus,
Babylon, Washington
1:15 P.M.

"Are you angry, Brian?" Trevor asked.

The words hung in the air, unanswered.

"Do you hate me?"

Nothing. But Trevor could see the hatred in Brian's dark blue eyes . . . the rage at being strapped to a cold metal table in this sterile classroom. *Poor Bri.* If only he understood that Trevor was trying to cure him, not kill him.

But none of Trevor's subjects ever understood that.

Then again, Trevor supposed that Brian had a good excuse to be angry. After all, Brian wasn't *supposed* to be here. Trevor had kicked him out of town in January. Brian's bad luck was almost comical. In Seattle he'd hooked up with a bunch of idiots who were driving south in an old bus. They became very lost in the rain—and ended up heading back north by accident. They drove straight to WIT in the middle of the night. Brian woke up one morning and found Trevor sticking a gun in his face. He had been trapped here ever since, alone and forgotten.

Forgotten until now, that is.

29

Trevor sighed. "Are you scared?" he asked.

The seconds ticked by in silence. Clearly Brian was too proud, too much of a *man* to give a reply. But the question was rhetorical, anyway. Of course he was scared. He was turning twenty-one in two days.

"We're wasting time," an impatient voice called from the hall. "Let's just leave him alone. I think we should check on Jezebel."

Trevor suppressed a scowl. *Relax, Barney.* Wasting time? Was that what he thought? Barney knew that cases like this one required constant observation. Both he and Trevor had witnessed hundreds of meltings. They knew that the plague could strike at any time in a two-month period—four weeks on either side of a twenty-first birthday. It rarely struck on the birthday itself. They *had* to keep watching. Besides, Jezebel was bound, gagged, and locked in the only secure cell in the entire building. For once she couldn't hurt herself or anyone else.

"Come on." Barney moaned.

Shut up, Trevor silently retorted. Barney probably just wanted to sneak a peek at Jezebel's underwear. He had the attention span of a laboratory rat. Come to think of it, he *looked* like a laboratory rat, with his round little eyes and hunched posture and tubby, chinless face. Yes. The analogy was fitting. *Rats.* All of Trevor's friends were rats. They were greedy weaklings who would sell each other out in an instant—just for a greater share of rations, or a chance at touching a beautiful girl, or a secret stash of home-made liquor. . . .

Trevor shook his head. There was no point in

getting worked up over a situation he couldn't change. His engineering school buddies were his only friends and allies in the postplague world—for better or worse.

He gazed down at the lab table. Brian's eyes remained fixed to the ceiling, poking through a wispy tangle of blond bangs. He wouldn't even so much as glance in Trevor's direction. The guy's defiance was pretty impressive. He might be a dolt, but he was tough. *Unlike* everybody else around here. Most kids would have long since succumbed to panic.

"No wonder Ariel likes you," Trevor said out loud. "No, wait, I'm sorry. No wonder she *liked* you. Past tense. She likes somebody else now. She told me she actually fell in love. Can you believe that? She's really changed. She never used to get so emotional. You know, unless she ran out of M&M's or something."

Brian's jaw twitched.

There you are. Trevor grinned slightly. So Brian did have a weak spot. He couldn't help but feel pleased. It wasn't that he enjoyed being cruel. No, no. Of course not. This was purely scientific. He simply wanted to hasten the onslaught of Brian's disease. A person nearing his twenty-first birthday would be more likely to vaporize if he were in a state of . . . well, *agitation*. And Trevor was anxious to get the process going, anxious to see if his latest theory worked. Time was short. His own twenty-first birthday was only fourteen months away. But he couldn't allow himself to think about that for too long. . . .

"I'm leaving," Barney grumbled. "We got better

things to do. Half the surveillance system is still down and—"

"Do you want to die?" Trevor interrupted.

There was a pause. "What?"

Trevor whirled around. "You heard me," he barked. "Do you want to die?"

Barney stood in the doorway, blinking. His pallid face sagged. "I—I just—"

"Because that's what'll happen if we walk away from this experiment," Trevor stated. "We'll never find a cure. We'll turn into black slime, just like everyone else. Is that what you want?"

"I just don't understand why we have to use *him*," Barney muttered sheepishly. "We don't know when he's gonna die. It could be today; it could be a month from now. It would be a lot easier if we used one of the kids with Chosen One syndrome. We know when *they* melt. We've seen it. They melt as soon as they start babbling about their visions. Always. And—"

"Thanks for telling me what I already know," Trevor cut in. "Now let me explain something to you. Let me tell you something you *don't* know. We're using Brian because you screwed up."

Barney's face reddened. "What—what are you talking about?" he stammered.

"Our last test subject vaporized this morning," Trevor spat. *"What?"* Barney cried. "But that's impossible. We have at least three more!"

Trevor shook his head in disgust. "For God's sake, when was the last time you actually bothered to *look* into one of the classrooms?" he demanded.

Barney stared at him idiotically. "I . . . I . . ."

"Remember the night you got drunk last week, Barney? Well, no—you probably don't. So let me explain it to you. You passed out, and that girl Leslie stole your keys. She let my sister out of her cell. But before she did that, she also let three more kids out of *theirs.*"

"Why didn't you tell me earlier?" Barney cried.

"Because I thought you might actually bother to *check,*" Trevor snapped. "You *are* part of my security detail. Or did you forget that, too?"

Barney ran a hand through his greasy hair. "I—I mean, that's what I was talking about," he muttered incoherently. "The surveillance system is down, so we have to repair it. We can't watch those classrooms anymore. . . ."

Incredible, Trevor thought. Barney still didn't grasp the gravity of the situation, the potential danger. If Trevor didn't cure Brian, they wouldn't have any more test subjects. Capturing a new one would be impossible. Ariel and her friend were obviously warning people to stay away from here. Besides, nobody made the mistake of wandering onto the WIT campus anymore, anyway—not after Trevor had slaughtered all of Ariel's friends. No, they were all hanging out together in a huge mob . . . where they were *safe.*

He supposed he could try to kidnap one of them. But no, that wouldn't work, either. Their numbers were too great. His supply of ammunition was growing thin. He couldn't even *keep* people here. He still hadn't repaired all the damage done by the locusts to the intricate system of cameras and television monitors. Gaping holes remained in his security.

Of course, if he cured Brian, all of his problems would be solved. The entire world would be in his debt—

"Trevor? Hey, Trevor."

Well, well. A smile crossed Trevor's face. So the boy could speak after all. Trevor turned back to the lab table.

"What is it?"

Brian swallowed. He still wouldn't make eye contact. He kept staring at the ceiling. His jaw was tightly set. "I just wanna know one thing," he snapped.

"Yeah?"

"How do you plan to cure me?"

Trevor's smile widened. "It's simple," he replied. He tapped the side of the table with a finger. "This surface is hooked to a generator. It's right under your back. As soon as you start exhibiting symptoms of the plague, I'm going to switch the power on and send a very low-level current of electricity through your body. Hopefully that will reverse the melting process."

Droplets of sweat appeared on Brian's forehead. "That's crazy," he whispered.

"It's a very minimal electric charge," Trevor said. "My experiments show that the substance remaining after a melting is nonconductive. Human tissue *is* conductive. So some sort of chemical reaction is taking place. . . . Well, I won't bore you with the details." He shrugged. "Anything else?"

Brian squirmed in the straps. "N-no," he stuttered. He coughed a few times. All at once his eyes widened. "It's just, I . . I don't feel so good," he choked out.

Trevor's eyes narrowed.

"Something's wrong." Brian moaned. His face grew flushed.

A small black bubble appeared on his cheek.

This is it! Trevor gasped. Terror and exhilaration washed over him. "Barney!" he shouted. "Barney, get in here!"

The bubble on Brian's face exploded in a small burst of blood and pus.

"Barney!" Trevor cried. "Get—"

Barney nearly knocked him over as he scrambled into the room.

Idiot! Scowling, Trevor ducked under the table and fumbled for the power switch. His breathing grew labored. This was no time for mistakes. The plague worked fast; every second counted. He grasped the black handle with trembling hands and pushed at it. It barely moved.

"Keep an eye on Brian," he said with a grunt. "Make sure the cables are all connected."

The switch snapped into position under the weight of Trevor's arm. There was a crack of blue light—and a searing pain stabbed through his fingers.

"Dammit!" he yelled. He jerked backward, falling over Barney's legs.

"Something's wrong!" Barney screamed. "Trevor! Something's wrong!"

Trevor staggered to his feet. *Oh, my God . . .*

What little remained of Brian's body was twitching wildly in a thick black and bloody mush. *Too much power,* Trevor thought wildly. *Something's malfunctioning!*

The electric current sizzled; the air was thick with smoke and the stench of ozone. Sparks flew everywhere. Instinctively Trevor threw up his hands and recoiled from the table.

"What's *happening?*" Barney shrieked.

And then the electricity died.

Just like that.

The room was silent.

"Jeez," Trevor muttered. He coughed and squinted in the haze, waving the smoke out of his eyes. Then he lowered his hands and peered tentatively at the table.

Oh, no.

Brian Landau was gone. A few burning shreds of his clothing lay in the steaming black ooze on the table, but that was it.

"Looks like we're back to square one," Barney stated in a colorless voice. "We don't understand this disease at all."

Trevor nodded. That was true, of course. But at that moment it didn't concern him nearly as much as the other consequence of the botched experiment.

No. Far more worrisome was that the last hope he had of saving *himself* had literally gone up in smoke.

FIVE

**Manhattan Bridge,
New York City
6:45 P.M.**

When Sarah awoke, she had no idea how long she'd been asleep. It might have been an hour. It might have been an entire *day*. She sat up and stretched. The sun was low in the sky, shining directly upon her through a tinted window. So . . . it was late afternoon. She was in the back of what had once been a bus. Most of the seats had been removed, and now the place looked like some kind of junkie's crash pad—complete with paint-splattered sofas and frayed carpets and candles. *Wow.* She must have been more exhausted than she realized. She hardly remembered coming in here.

"How do you feel?" Darrell asked.

Sarah jumped. He was sitting in a worn easy chair right beside her. And Aviva lay on a couch nearby, sound asleep, snoring softly.

"Sorry," he murmured with an apologetic grin. "I didn't mean to scare you."

"No, no—that's okay." She leaned back into the seat cushion and tried to smile. "I'm just, uh . . . a little out of it."

"I'll bet," Darrell said. "You guys were really beat. Where were you coming from?"

37

Sarah sighed. "Egypt," she said.

"Egypt?" His eyes narrowed. "As in the country?"

"Yeah," she croaked. She rubbed her eyes, then fumbled through her jeans pocket for her glasses. "It's kind of a long story."

"How did you . . . ?" He left the question hanging.

"We came over on a boat," she explained tiredly. "We heard that America was some kind of paradise. But when we got here, we were swarmed with all these grasshoppers and—"

"Locusts," Darrell interrupted.

Sarah paused. "What?"

"Not grasshoppers. Locusts." He flashed another grin. "Sorry. Go on."

Sarah's face shriveled. *Locusts?* The last time she'd heard anybody mention locusts was in Hebrew school—in discussions about the Torah and the plagues of Egypt.

"Sarah?" he prodded.

"Sorry." She swallowed. "Anyway, the boat sank. A lot of people died. Aviva and I are the only ones left."

"Wow," Darrell mumbled. "I . . . I didn't know." He looked at her closely. "What were you doing in Egypt in the first place?"

"I was going to college in Israel. I kind of wound up in Egypt by accident—" The last words stuck in her throat. *Okay.* Time to change the subject. If she thought any more about Egypt, she'd start thinking about Ibrahim—and then she'd lose control of herself. She waved her hand toward the window. "So what is this place?" she asked quickly.

Darrell shrugged. "The Manhattan Bridge," he said.

She managed a laugh. "No kidding. But why are you *living* on it?"

"Just kind of ended up here, I guess." He shook his head. "For a long time Manhattan wasn't very safe. Most kids I know figured they'd be safer on a bridge. That's what *I* figured. There are only two ways on and off. It made sense. We could protect ourselves."

Sarah felt a shiver of apprehension. "Protect yourselves from what?"

He sneered. "The pigs."

Pigs? Sarah blinked. "Darrell, you're going to have to start from the top. I've been away for a long time. Since before New Year's. I'm sorry—"

"No, no, it's my fault. I'm talking about the government. The good old US of A. They're the dangerous ones."

Sarah's eyes widened. "The government?"

He nodded, lowering his eyes. "Yup. After the blackout and the plague, they spent a couple of months going through Manhattan with machine guns. Killing everyone they saw."

"Are you *serious?*" she cried. "Why?"

"Beats me," he grumbled. "All I know is that they were hell-bent on mowing down as many of us as possible. It was weird, though. They had these soldiers dressed up like monks in black robes. And a lot of them were girls. I mean, like, *our* age. Isn't that sick?"

Sarah felt the blood drain from her face.

Girls in black robes. That was sick, all right. She

suddenly felt as if she were about to vomit. She knew all about those girls. Back in January four of them showed up at her granduncle's doorstep in Jerusalem, looking for the scroll. And when they didn't find it, they blew his house to bits. They knew everything about him, too—including the fact that he had a grandniece in Tel Aviv. *Her*.

"You should've seen what it was like," he went on. "The whole city was a mess. But then they just disappeared. One day they were here, the next they were gone." He laughed coldly. "Most of the kids in the city still like to stay on the bridge, though. There are kids on the Brooklyn and Williamsburg Bridges, too, and—"

"Did you ever talk to any of them?" Sarah cut in. "I mean, the girls in black robes? Do you have any idea what they wanted?"

He shook his head. "No." He hesitated. "But . . . there is one thing. After New Year's Eve a lot of kids started talking about some kind of savior, a Chosen One." He drew in his breath. "Those kids were the first to get shot."

Oh, no. Sarah gripped the edge of her seat, struggling to remain calm. "How . . . how do you know it was the government?" she choked out.

"Who else could it have been?" Darrell snorted. "They had guns. They had helicopters. I figure they hated the way things were turning out in this country. They wanted to start over. So they dropped the plague on us and . . ."

Sarah couldn't listen anymore. *Okay, okay*. She had to relax. Those girls were gone. Besides, they

40

didn't know that *she* was the Chosen One. They only knew that she was Elijah's grandniece. Back in Jerusalem, she'd overheard them saying that she was of "no importance." But that was a long time ago. They might have learned what she had learned since then: namely, that the scroll's prophecies were about *her*. Anything was possible. She couldn't afford to take any chances. None.

So she would just forget about being the Chosen One. Yes. If she didn't mention it, nobody would ever find out. Right? She would make sure that Aviva never mentioned it, either. Or maybe she would just let Aviva go west without her. That was a good idea: Aviva could go west, and *she* would stay with Darrell. Forever. Where she would be safe. Where she would be protected.

". . . last time I was in Manhattan was probably three months ago," Darrell was saying. "The pigs were all gone. . . ."

Pigs. He was talking about the black-robed girls. But were they really with the government? She just couldn't believe it. The girls in Jerusalem had spoken with *English* accents. So who were they? What did they want—besides the scroll? She chewed on her lip. At least the scroll was at the bottom of the harbor, beyond their reach. . . .

"Sarah?" Darrell asked. "Did you hear what I just said?"

She glanced up at him. "No," she mumbled.

He smiled. "It's okay. I just wanted to know where you heard that America was a paradise. I mean, who told you?"

41

She shrugged. "Everybody, really. There was a rumor floating around the ship. And we kept on picking up these commercials on our radio—"

"Hold on," Darrell interrupted. He hopped out of his chair and trotted up to the front of the bus. "I want you to hear something." A cheap, dust-covered boom box sat on the dashboard. He snatched it up by the handle, then headed back to the seat and flicked the power switch. Soft static flowed from the speakers as he slumped down into the cushions. He began twisting the dial slowly, slowly. . . .

"Now *dat's* what I'm tawkin' about," a man's distorted voice said.

Sarah gasped.

"That's it!" she cried. She couldn't believe it. It was the *same* ad—the one she'd already heard a million times on the boat. She leaned forward and peered at the radio band. The little red line was poised just over the number 100. Sarah made a face. She used to listen to this station all the time in high school.

"Ever been to the Empire State Building?" Darrell suddenly asked, turning off the box.

The Empire State Building? Sarah shook her head. What did *that* have to do with anything?

"See, we've been hearing this stuff, too," he said. "Ever since January. The signal is coming from the Empire State Building—remember the ad for that station? 'From the top of the Empire State Building . . .'"

Sarah gasped. She'd forgotten all about it.

"I was thinking about going and checking it out. Plus from there it's a bird's-eye view of the whole

42

city, so I can see how many people moved back to Manhattan." He raised his eyebrows. "You wanna come with me?"

She stared at him. "You mean . . . now?" she asked, baffled.

He laughed quietly. "No. Of course not. Whenever. After you get some rest and eat a couple of good meals. I just thought you might be curious."

"Um, okay," she said uncertainly.

"You aren't planning on leaving anytime soon, are you?" he asked. " 'Cause, you know, you're welcome to stay here as long as you want."

"I don't ever want to leave," she blurted out. *Uh-oh*. Maybe that was a little too pushy. "I mean, if that's okay."

"Of course it's okay," he murmured.

Thank God.

"Hey—speaking of food, are you hungry?" he asked. He set the box down on the floor and pushed himself out of the chair. "I was thinking about rustling up a bite. I got a friend who makes kick-ass Rice Krispies treats."

Sarah nodded. "Sure," she whispered.

"Great. You can just hang here. I'll be back." He smiled at her one last time, then turned and disappeared out the front door.

Sarah eased back in her chair and sighed deeply. So it was settled. Warm relief coursed through her veins. Who would have thought that she'd be happy to spend the rest of her life hanging out on the Manhattan Bridge with Darrell Ewing? Then again, who would have thought that her friends and family would have melted away into puddles of black slime?

The point was, she could finally stop wandering. She could finally stop searching for the answers to some strange puzzle she would never solve. The burden had been lifted. She didn't have to worry anymore. There was nothing left to do—nothing to do but wait until *her* time came to melt.

She was home.

PART II

June 2-20

SIX

Amarillo,
Texas
Early morning, June 4

Julia Morrison sat alone at the edge of a locust-eaten cornfield, gazing eastward as the sun began to climb over the Promised Land. *Another sunrise, another day without George. That makes twelve.*

She'd been up before dawn every single morning since she'd last seen him. The twelve days were more like twelve *months*, a year, twelve years . . . a lifetime. She couldn't seem to sleep for longer than two hours at a stretch, and even those brief naps were fitful and marked by nightmares. Every time she dozed, she would wake up in a cold sweat—gripped by a longing for George so profound that she would actually cry out in pain.

Yet she understood why the Healer had to keep George apart from her. Yes, in spite of how much it hurt, she knew the reasons. George had committed a crime. True . . . *she* secretly felt that his crime wasn't all that great. He'd just told one little lie. He'd put on a show, really. A small charade in a sad effort to convince her that the Healer wasn't the Chosen One. He hadn't acted out of hatred for the Healer, either. He had acted out of love for *her.*

47

But the Healer was compassionate and forgiving. George Porter wasn't a criminal. George was just a boy—a desperate, broken boy for whom lying had often been the only solution in a troubled past. His reasons weren't evil or sinister. He only wanted to leave this place so that he could be alone with Julia again, like he had been for those two short months of spring, when their love first blossomed. . . .

It was so easy back then.

Julia's eyes brimmed with tears. She didn't even know why she still went through the motions of crying. She should be impervious to misery by now. After all, misery was her constant companion, her only friend. She'd known nothing but loss for three straight years. First her parents, then her home, then her friends—and then, of course, the *world.*

Still, she had the Healer. Even though he was depriving her of the boy she loved, he had given her a place to live and new hope for the world. And she knew that in spite of George's mistakes, she still had *him,* too. The boy who understood her completely. The soul mate who was haunted by visions like hers, who felt the pull west like she did. . . .

The father of my unborn child.

She rubbed her taut belly under the folds of her grubby white robe. At least she didn't *look* pregnant. Her secret was safely hidden—for a while, anyway. She had the same bony frame she'd always had. Still, on mornings like these, her smooth brown skin might be a little puffy, and her deep brown eyes might be ringed with dark circles. But she could pass that off as exhaustion—

Uh-oh.

A rushing noise filled her ears. She blinked. The sound grew louder, and the next moment she was overcome by a familiar, dizzying vertigo. Her body seemed to list to one side.

A vision was coming.

She fought back the flutter of fear. She had to relax. There was no reason to be scared. None at all. How many times had this happened? A hundred? The daylight grew dimmer and dimmer. . . .

I can't see! The desert sun is blindingly bright. The sword is in my hand, but I can't find the Demon. I know it's near me. I can hear its laughter. I can smell its foul breath. But if I can't see it, I can't kill it. It will get me first—

"Julia?"

She opened her eyes.

Someone stood over her. She brushed her long, matted brown curls out of her face—then drew in her breath.

The Healer. His long mane of dark hair and broad shoulders seemed to perfectly eclipse the sun. The backlighting cast the outline of his face in a radiant aura. *It's like a halo,* she thought. Yes. A manifestation of his holiness. A tremendous feeling of warmth suddenly flowed out from her. She sniffed and wiped her cheek. He had saved her from the Demon. And soon he would return George to her. Everything was going to be okay.

"Are you all right?" he asked.

"Fine," she murmured. "I just had a vision."

He bent close to her. "What's wrong?"

"I—I don't know," she stammered. "I guess I'm just worried about George." She hesitated. "Is it . . . is it okay if I see him? I mean I know he has to be alone, but it's been a long time."

The Healer blinked. His smile remained intact, but his glittering blue eyes darkened. "George is no longer a concern of yours, Julia," he whispered.

No longer a concern? Julia shook her head. How could he say that? He *knew* what she felt for George. "But—"

"You have to forget about George," he interrupted, softly but firmly. "He violated my commandments. So you have to move on with your life. Your *real* life. As a Visionary. As a prized member of the flock."

"But I can't move on without George," she protested. "I mean, can't I just see him? I don't even have to talk to him—"

"That's enough," the Healer snapped. He straightened. "You can't see him because I say so. My word is law. My word is final."

Julia's eyes began to water again. She couldn't help herself. Why was the Healer being so cruel? It wasn't like him. Even convicted murderers, even prisoners on death row—even *they* were allowed to have visitors. So why couldn't she see George? Unless . . .

No.

She shoved the black thought from her mind. There was no *way* the Healer could have hurt George. The Healer didn't hurt nonbelievers. She'd heard stories . . . there was a girl named Larissa who'd betrayed him. And she was still alive. Julia had *seen* her.

"Ju-just tell me something," she choked out. "Is George okay?"

The Healer lowered his eyes. "No more questions about the boy," he growled.

A chill shot up Julia's spine. Why wouldn't he answer? Why was he avoiding her gaze?

"Listen, Julia, I know you're upset," he said after a moment. He softened his tone. "But you have to clear your mind. I'm introducing a new rule, and I want you to be the first to know about it."

Julia gaped at him. He wouldn't even *talk* about George. *No, no, no. Something terrible must have happened. . . .*

"We're embarking on a glorious new era of the Promised Land," the Healer stated. "We're going to plant new crops and turn this place into a Garden of Eden before we head west and confront the Demon. To help us along, I'm asking that each member of the flock form a partnership with another member—a special bond that will enable everyone to encourage each other. Each will remain at the other's side."

Why? she wondered miserably. Why was he doing this? It made no sense. Julia already had a special bond with somebody. She had a partner. If she could be with George, everything would be fine. She would make George see the error of his ways. So why was the Healer torturing her? After everything he'd provided, after all the miracles he'd performed, why did he have to lash out at somebody who loved him and trusted him so much?

"I want you to team up with Linda Altman," he went on. "You two are among my most valued followers. I want you to show every disciple of mine that if two people work together, they can become far more than the sum of their parts."

She shook her head. "Did you hurt him?" she whispered. "Is that why you're putting me with Linda instead of George? Did you do something—"

"Enough!" Harold raged. "I'm *healing* George, Julia! Don't you understand? When I'm through with him . . . well, he won't be the same person he was. Believe me. You won't even recognize him anymore. It's best just to put him out of your mind."

"But *why?*" she wailed.

He looked her directly in the eye. "Because the old George Porter is *gone*, Julia. Forever."

SEVEN

**New York City
Night of June 5**

After only five days Sarah pretended she was fit enough to accompany Darrell to the Empire State Building. But the truth was that she could have rested for about five months. She wasn't all that excited to leave the bridge, either, even for such a short stroll. She felt so *comfortable* here, so at home—with the bustling crowd, the kids who partied and sang songs and haggled over food and clothing. The noisy atmosphere reminded her so much of the way New York City used to be. It was like an endless street fair.

Really, she just wanted to get away from Aviva.

The girl was starting to seriously annoy her. She wouldn't shut up about how they had to leave, about how they had to go west. Fine. If Aviva wanted to go west, she should just *go*. But she also refused to leave Sarah behind. Why couldn't she just accept the fact that Sarah wasn't going anywhere?

At least Aviva kept her visions to herself. And so far, she'd kept her promise about not telling anyone that Sarah was the Chosen One. But how long would that last? Every day Aviva grew more antsy

53

and agitated, whining incessantly in Sarah's ear . . . like an annoying pet.

Well, she's not here now, Sarah reminded herself as she followed Darrell down the long slope of the bridge to the Lower East Side of Manhattan. *So just forget about it.*

The sun had long since set. In the fading dusk the drab brick buildings of Chinatown and Little Italy seemed to turn quickly from red to dark gray. There was a steady, singsong rattle: the chirping of crickets. It suddenly occurred to Sarah that she had never heard crickets in Manhattan before. Their presence was somehow ominous . . . a hint that despite outward appearances, the city really *had* changed. It was no longer civilized. It was a dead wilderness.

"You all right?" Darrell asked.

She nodded.

"Look, I know it's kind of creepy to go at night," he apologized. "It's just easier to tell if people are around when it's dark. They light fires. Fires are harder to see in the daytime. I figure from the top of the Empire State Building, we'll be able to see every fire in the city."

Sarah shrugged. "I don't mind," she murmured. She hadn't minded until *now,* anyway.

By the time they reached the intersection of Canal and Mott Streets, night had fallen completely. Darrell stopped short.

"What is it?" Sarah whispered.

He frowned and glanced to his right. Then he sniffed. "That smell," he muttered, wrinkling his nose. "It stinks around here. You smell it?"

Sarah took a quick whiff of the balmy night air. *Yuck.* Something *did* stink. The odor was thick and fetid, like a refrigerator full of rotting meat. She glanced around. There was an abandoned Chinese restaurant on the northeast corner. Her lips twisted in disgust.

Darrell pulled a flashlight from the pocket of his windbreaker. "It's coming from down there," he said, nodding toward Mott Street.

Sarah squinted into the blackness. She couldn't see a thing—only uncertain shadows and dark, shapeless mounds. The prickling anxiety in her stomach crept up a notch. Darrell flicked the switch—

Her throat constricted.

She started shaking her head—desperately, uncontrollably.

God, no. It can't be real. It isn't real. . . .

Mott Street was piled high with mutilated kids.

Once, back at journalism school, Sarah had been assigned to watch a movie called *The Killing Fields.* And there was one grisly scene that had haunted her ever since. . . . A reporter was struggling to flee a bloody civil war in Cambodia. He slipped in a rice paddy and found himself face-to-face with a corpse. Horror dawned on him as he looked one way, then another, and suddenly realized he was surrounded by dozens of dead bodies. He had inadvertently stumbled upon a mass grave.

Sarah burst into tears when she saw it. It was one of the few times in her life when she'd completely lost control of herself. But even that gruesome image of death, that sea of bones and rotting flesh—even *that* was nothing compared to the sheer carnage that greeted her eyes now.

There were hundreds of bodies. Maybe thousands. The flashlight couldn't possibly illuminate them all. A massacre of unfathomable proportions had taken place here. And these people hadn't only been *killed;* they'd been torn limb from limb.

"I had no idea," Darrell whispered.

Sarah screamed. The shrill sound pierced the stillness, echoing off the empty buildings—

"Shhh," Darrell whispered. He grabbed her and squeezed her tightly against him. "Shhh, Sarah, it's okay. It's okay. We're safe. It's like I said. They're not around here anymore. This happened a long time ago."

"Maybe we should go back," she sobbed. "Maybe . . ."

"Go ahead," Darrell said. His voice was soothing. "Just head straight back up the bridge. It's not far. About a half mile. You'll be safe. Go on."

Sarah pressed her face against his chest. "What about you?"

He shook his head. "I'm gonna keep going," he said.

"Bu-but that's crazy," she stammered. "You could get killed and—"

"No, I won't. I promise. Whoever did this is long gone."

A tear fell from Sarah's cheek. "How do you *know?*"

"Because I live here, Sarah," he replied gently. He took a deep breath and stepped away from her. "Look, I'm not suicidal or anything. This freaks me out, too. But I wouldn't put myself in danger. I want to *live,* okay?"

Sarah swallowed. "You sure it's safe?"

"Positive." He waved the flashlight back toward the bridge. "But I understand if you don't want to come."

Sniffling, Sarah glanced back down Canal Street. She couldn't even see the bridge from here. It couldn't be *that* close. The thought of walking with Darrell through Manhattan was terrifying—but the thought of walking *alone,* even for a half mile, was simply unacceptable.

"It's all right," she whispered. "I'll come with you."

The next two hours passed in a fog. Sarah kept her eyes closed most of the time, leaning against Darrell, fighting to keep from simply collapsing with fright. Darrell kept one arm wrapped tightly around her shoulders throughout the entire walk. She supposed they must have passed more bodies because every now and then he seemed to veer off from the straight course and take a circuitous route.

And then he stopped.

"We're here," he whispered.

Already? She opened her eyes. They were standing in front of a revolving door. She lifted her head and squinted toward the night sky. Sure enough, an immense skyscraper loomed over her, but it was so close that she couldn't even see the building's signature needle on top. Rows and rows of familiar-looking art deco windows seemed to stretch off into infinity.

"Ready for a hike?" Darrell asked, trying his best

to sound cheerful. "It's eighty-six floors to the observation deck."

"Okay," Sarah whispered. But her voice was hollow. Her heart began to pound.

Darrell turned on the flashlight once more—*click*—then pushed through the doors and into the pitch blackness of the lobby. Sarah forced herself to follow him.

The vast, low-ceilinged room was dusty and empty, void of furnishings or people. At least *that* was a relief. Part of her half expected to be riddled with bullets the moment she stepped inside. The dim yellow beam of light danced jerkily across the walls and came to rest on a door marked Stairwell. Darrell glanced at her.

She nodded. There was nothing more to say. Without a word, they hurried through the door and began to climb—with only the shaky light of the flashlight to guide them.

At first Sarah's idea was to ascend as quickly as possible. She kept her eyes pinned to Darrell's ankles as she marched, up and up. Their footsteps reverberated off the dark concrete. But after several minutes she began having trouble breathing. She fell a few feet behind him. Her head swam as she rounded the corners again and again and again. And she couldn't help but think: *Wait a second. What am I even doing here? What do I care if there are people living in Manhattan or not?*

"Sarah?" Darrell asked. His lungs were heaving. "You okay?"

"Fine," she croaked. "I just . . . I just need a little break."

Ten seconds, maybe twenty—and they were off again. Floor after floor, flight after flight of stairs . . . Sarah's knees began to burn. Her bones ached. An eternity passed. She felt as if her chest were filled with hot smoke. She took another little rest. . . .

"Come on," Darrell urged. "It's not too much farther."

Gasping for breath, she resumed her plodding climb. She no longer focused on anything but the passing numbers at each landing.

Eighty-four . . . eighty-five . . .

"Here it is," Darrell announced breathlessly.

Sarah just stared at him. She didn't have the energy to answer. Purple dots swam before her eyes. She scampered up the last few steps on all fours, using her hands to carry her weight. Darrell hauled her to her feet at the landing. She couldn't seem to catch her breath. She couldn't believe she'd actually climbed eighty-six floors. Eighty-six . . . But Darrell didn't waste any time. He swiftly escorted her around a corner and down a long, narrow corridor—then paused in front of a heavy steel door.

"This is it," he whispered. He glanced at her. "Ready?"

She paused, swallowing. *Not really. I can't even breathe—*

He pushed open the door with his foot. A blast of chilly wind swept over Sarah's face, rustling her hair. Darrell tiptoed out onto the promenade, glanced to his left—and froze.

"Whoa," he mumbled. He scowled and lowered the flashlight.

"What is it?" she whispered.

He shook his head. "Come take a look at this."

Summoning the shredded remnants of her energy and courage, she stepped through the door and followed his gaze. *What on earth . . .*

Somebody had built a *fire* up here. Right in the middle of the deck. A huge pile of charred wood was surrounded by seven identical, spherical stones—maybe two feet in diameter. Darrell's flashlight swept over them. Sarah narrowed her eyes. Arcane symbols had been painted on each of the stones: the outline of a female body, a bird of some kind . . . and next to the circle was a huge white radar dish, aimed straight at the tip of the Empire State Building's antenna. On it, a single word had been painted in letters three feet tall:

LILITH

That name! Sarah's stomach squeezed. It was the same name the black-robed girls had invoked in Jerusalem. They'd burned Elijah's house to cinders as an "offering" to . . . *that.*

"I—I've heard of Lilith," she stammered, horrified.

Darrell nodded, frowning. "Yeah. Me too."

She turned to him. "You *have?*"

"Yeah." He laughed humorlessly. "I always wondered why they named that rock tour after a demon. You know, Lilith Fair? It seems kind of weird—"

"Wait," she interrupted. Her throat was suddenly very dry. "Did you say *'demon'?*"

"Yeah." His forehead wrinkled. "Why? What's wrong?"

"Lilith is a demon?" Sarah whispered in a quavering voice.

"Well, that's what the legend is." He sighed. "She was actually supposed to be Adam's first wife, even before Eve. Then she was kicked out of the Garden of Eden. So she became a demon, with all sorts of evil powers. Nobody really knows much about her. She's only mentioned in the Bible once, in this apocalyptic text. It says she lives in the desert. Some people say that the 'desert' really means like a state of limbo—and that Lilith is supposed to come back at the end of time as, like, this vampire." He snorted. "It's all a bunch of crap. But looking at this, I guess *somebody* believes in it."

Sarah stared at him, flabbergasted. *Apocalyptic text?* He sounded as if he were quoting an encyclopedia. "Where did you learn all that?" she asked.

He shrugged. "Seminary school."

Sarah's jaw dropped. For a moment she forgot everything—even her fear. "You were going to be a *priest?*"

"A Baptist minister." He flashed a melancholy smile. "You sound shocked."

She blinked. *Oops.* "Well, uh, no . . . uh, it's just, uh—"

"I knew I was either going to be a minister or a politician," he mumbled. "But I kind of lost my taste for politics after senior year of high school."

Her mouth hung slack. She couldn't believe it. She'd been completely wrong about Darrell. *Completely.* "I'm sorry," she whispered, as if that would even make a difference.

"It's all right," he murmured in a faraway voice. "Politics was never my bag. I guess I also sort of lost my faith in a lot of other things."

Much to Sarah's surprise, tears began to well in her eyes. *That sounds like something Ibrahim would have said.* She'd been wrong about Ibrahim, too. At first she'd thought he was cold and heartless and crazy. But he and Darrell were actually a lot alike. Both were very strong. And they were also very lost. Both had believed in something deeply, only to have their beliefs shattered by *them*—these mysterious Demon worshipers, for reasons still unknown. . . .

"I don't think these people are with the government," Darrell muttered. "It's deeper than that. It has to do with the Chosen One . . . if there is one. They don't want anyone to find him."

Sarah shot him a frightened glance. "What do you mean?"

"Think about it. The kids who talked about the Chosen One were trying to go west. But these Lilith people must have rigged up this radio signal so that everyone would come *here* instead." He frowned at the radar dish. "It's like a decoy . . . a trap. It's got to be."

"A—A trap?" she stammered. "But why?"

"Who knows? Maybe something is going to happen out west that they don't want people to know about. Maybe they killed all those kids as a warning to everyone else who shows up in town. Like: 'Try to go west and you'll end up like them.' Yeah." He nodded. *"They* probably left to go out west, too."

My God. Sarah's blood ran cold. Of course. It made perfect sense. Something *was* going to happen out west. That was why Aviva was being such a pain in the neck. She still felt the "pull" that all the other Visionaries had talked about on the ship.

But Sarah didn't feel it. She didn't have visions. So she could be trapped. Obviously she *had* been trapped—by the very people she wanted so badly to forget: those black-robed girls. It was all so clear now, so sickening. The followers of Lilith had drawn her to New York with the stupid radio commercials, and fear had kept her here. . . .

Sarah scowled. *Not anymore. I won't let them beat me.*

A burning terror inside her was growing, yet so was a fierce resolve—a *fury* she hadn't experienced since she'd been blasted out of Elijah's house in Israel. She felt as if she were waking up from a long sleep. She wasn't going to be manipulated or out-smarted. No way.

I'm the Chosen One.

Yes. The few, brief days of hiding from herself were over. Even though she no longer had the scroll, she had a *duty* to fight back as best she could. She owed it to Aviva, to Ibrahim, to every Visionary she'd ever met. Besides, Darrell had taken her a step closer toward solving at least part of the riddle. Now she knew that Lilith and the "Demon" of the scroll were the same. And despite Darrell's dismissal of the legend, there *was* truth in it. Lilith was very real. According to the last prophecy Sarah had read before the shipwreck, Lilith was out among the survivors of the plague, disguised in human form. Somewhere . . .

Unconsciously Sarah's eyes wandered out over the city. The bottom half of Manhattan stretched far below her—triangular and black as ebony, with the water on either side glistening like a pair of curved swords under the starry sky. There wasn't a single light among all the buildings . . . except for the bridges across the East River, blazing with the flickering red glow of a hundred fires. *So much for finding more kids in Manhattan,* she thought grimly. Those meager flames represented the last of what had once been a metropolis of millions. Lilith and her followers had seen to that.

"What are you thinking?" Darrell asked in the silence.

"I'm thinking that I'm going to head west," Sarah said simply. "I'm going to find Lilith. I'm going to try to figure out what the hell is going on."

Amarillo,
Texas
Morning of June 7

For three whole days and nights Julia managed to keep her suspicions and fears about George a secret. She worked alongside Linda Altman in silence—planting new crops in the fields, sweeping away the remains of the locusts, cleaning the barn. The Healer seemed very pleased at the success of the partnership. And if he was pleased . . . well, then maybe he would let her ask about George again. Maybe she would find out the truth.

Maybe.

At least she had been paired with Linda. At this point Linda was probably the closest thing Julia even had to a friend. She loved the musical sound of Linda's British accent, her quick wit and easygoing humor. Even Linda's face was enough to make Julia smile, with those blond curls and wry smile and bright blue eyes. . . .

I should talk to her, Julia thought as she scattered corn seed by the side of the dusty road that led out of the Promised Land. After all, she and Linda were alone. The rest of the flock was on the other side of the barn. *I can't keep this inside anymore. The more I hold it in, the angrier I get at the Healer—*

"What's wrong, Julia?" Linda murmured.

Julia stiffened. *Is it that obvious?* "I . . ." She bit her lip. "Nothing."

Linda chuckled softly. "It has to be *something.* You've been seeding that same spot for the past twenty minutes."

Julia stared at the ground. She had to laugh. Linda was right. It didn't take a mind reader to know that Julia wasn't herself. A sloppy mound of yellow pellets covered her worn sneakers. She hadn't even realized that she was standing still.

"You *can* talk to me, you know," Linda went on. "I told you that, remember? Besides, we're partners. The Healer wants us to share."

"I know," Julia mumbled, swallowing. She glanced at Linda, then back at the earth. "I just . . . I'm not good at sharing, I guess."

Linda smiled sadly. "You've had a hard lot of it, haven't you?"

Julia sighed. "No. I mean, I don't know. I don't want to feel sorry for myself or anything. But for so long, I was used to hiding everything I felt. I was used to putting on an act. I guess it just became . . . natural." She shook her head. What was she even *talking* about?

"Why did you have to hide things?" Linda asked.

"Well, I didn't *always* have to hide things," Julia said. "Mostly with Luke. My old boyfriend. He . . . ah, he wasn't the most understanding guy in the world. He used to hit me all the time and call me names and stuff." She suddenly found she was clenching her fists at her sides. Her voice became strained. "He even tried to get George killed. Remember how I told you about those girls we met in Ohio, back in February? The ones who had that weird house and were into devil worship or whatever? They said that they wanted to kill all the Visionaries. And Luke *told* them that George had visions."

Linda didn't say anything for a while. "I'm sorry," she finally whispered.

"Forget it." Julia shook her head, thrusting Luke from her mind. She didn't even know why she'd thought about him in the first place. "Listen, Linda—if I tell you something, will you *promise* you won't tell a soul?"

"Of course," Linda answered emphatically. "You don't even need to ask."

Julia took a deep breath. "I'm worried the Healer did something to George."

Linda frowned. "I don't understand."

"I'm worried he hurt him."

Linda's expression cleared, and she laughed. "That's crazy!" Julia raised her head. "Then why won't he let me see him?"

"Oh, Julia . . ." Linda sighed. "George is fine. He just needs to be by himself. The Healer wants him to think about what he's done. Alone. It's going to take a while, okay? You have to be patient."

"But how do you *know* he's all right?" Julia pressed, her voice rising.

Linda leaned forward and took Julia's hand in her own. "Because I *saw* him. Julia, listen to me. You have to stop worrying. George is in the basement of the main house. I was just there yesterday."

Julia blinked. "You were?"

Linda laughed again. *"Yes!"* she cried. "And as soon as he realizes what an ass he's been, you'll see him again."

"But . . . but . . ." Julia's brow grew furrowed. She supposed she was relieved, but part of her was baffled—even angry. Why had *Linda* been allowed to see him? Did the Healer *want* Julia to think that something bad had happened to George? Was the Healer playing some kind of mind game with her? It wasn't right—

"Now why don't you tell me what's really wrong," Linda murmured. She squeezed Julia's hand tightly. "Okay?"

Julia's body tensed. "What do you mean?"

"I know that something else is bothering you," she stated gently. "Something other than George. Whatever it is, it's been bothering you for a long time now. Before George was taken away."

Oh, no. Julia abruptly withdrew her hand. She suddenly felt very hot. "Nothing . . . uh, I mean, I'm fine."

"Julia?" Linda whispered. "Whatever you tell me will stay between us. I swear I won't tell a soul."

Julia averted her eyes. She held her breath. Did Linda know about the pregnancy? No—that was impossible. But sooner or later, people would find out. Besides, the secret was festering inside Julia, tormenting her, tearing her apart. And she knew she would *have* to tell somebody when her condition became obvious. She still hadn't told George, though. He deserved to be the first to know. He had a *right*. But she might not even see him again until it was too late. . . .

After what seemed like an eternity, she exhaled. She kept staring at the ground. "You give me your word?" she asked in a hollow voice.

"I give you my word," Linda promised.

Julia opened her mouth. The words wouldn't come. She'd never actually admitted this out loud, even to herself. But she squeezed her eyes shut and fought to continue. It *would* feel good to confide in someone. Besides, it wasn't as if Julia had done anything wrong. She hadn't violated any of Harold's rules. Well . . . at least, not in the Promised Land. Commandment five prohibited sexual relations—but she hadn't had any with George *here*. That was what counted. She'd barely even *kissed* him since they left Illinois.

"I'm pregnant," Julia finally spat.

She opened her eyes and glanced up at Linda.

Linda's face turned a chalky white. "Oh, my God," she murmured. "Julia . . ."

Julia smiled sadly. *So much for feeling better,* she thought. Her eyes moistened again. "George doesn't know," she choked out. "He's the father."

"I had no idea." Linda swallowed. "When did you . . . when did you find out?"

"Not too long ago," she whispered tremulously. She rubbed her moist eyes and shook her head. "Maybe a month."

Linda ran a hand through her hair. "Are you sure you don't want to tell the Healer?"

Julia nodded vigorously. "Positive. Nobody can know."

"Julia, you need to forget about George," Linda said softly. She reached out and gently massaged Julia's shoulder. "He wouldn't have made a good father, anyway—"

"What?" Julia wailed. She jerked away from Linda's hand. "You don't know him! How can you even talk to me like that? Do you know how much that kills me?"

Linda's face fell. She looked pained. "I'm just telling you what I think," she said in a pleading voice. "I just think that you should put your trust in the Healer."

"But I can't! That's the whole—" Julia hesitated. A car was coming down the road from the main highway. She peered at it as it bounced toward them through the dirt. Even from a distance she could tell that it was packed with people. *More arrivals,* she thought with a strange sense of foreboding. *More kids who've heard the rumors and hope to be saved from the plague. I wonder if any of them are pregnant, too.*

She squinted at the car. Four kids sat crammed into the front seat. She could plainly see their faces in the morning sun. *Good Lord.* One of them looked a lot like—

She nearly screamed.

No!

The car roared past Julia and vanished in a cloud of dust. Blood turned to ice in her veins. She must be hallucinating. How could *he* be *here?* He should be dead. He was already twenty-one. His birthday was last month! It was impossible!

"Julia?" Linda asked.

She barely heard the word. Her mind was very, very far away. So was the pregnancy. And George. And everything else that mattered. Because even in that split second, she knew it was *him*. It had been so many months . . . but that face was still as familiar to her as her own. It had grown more haggard, more emaciated—but it was the same. The same hard jaw-line. The same ice blue eyes and greasy black hair. And she hadn't made the connection until now, but in some ways his face looked a lot like the Healer's. But the handsome features were somehow perverted, made twisted and ugly and evil. . . .

"Don't ever try to run away from me again. If you do, I'll kill you. Got it?"

"What is it, Julia?" Linda demanded. There was an edge of panic in her voice. "Julia! What's the matter?"

"It's my old boyfriend," Julia gasped. "The one I was telling you about. It's Luke."

Amarillo,
Texas
Night of June 7

For many weeks now Dr. Harold Wurf had been riding a wave of unparalleled success. His awesome powers had driven the locusts from the Promised Land. His wrath had crushed the will of every nonbeliever. Even George Porter, that loudmouthed juvenile delinquent—even *he* was finally broken, lying in abject sorrow on the cold floor of Harold's dank cellar. Soon he would learn to love Harold, too. Every day word of Harold's miracles and divine wonders spread like fire, drawing more and more lost teenage souls to him. His flock had nearly doubled since the expulsion of the locusts.

He *was* the Healer. The Chosen One. The savior of the plague survivors.

So why is this happening? he wondered. The absence of his two favorite females defied logic. It enraged him. He paced back and forth across the creaky, straw-covered barn floor, deliberately avoiding the eyes of the eighteen others present. *Why am I being forsaken? By them! By the two I love most!*

He avoided the temptation to glance at his watch.

There was no point; he was well aware that this meeting should have started an hour ago. Each week the Visionaries of the Promised Land gathered here in a circle to talk by candlelight—at the *same* time, on the *same* night. Without fail. It was a tradition, a ritual. It was *important*. Julia and Linda knew that. They cherished it. So where were they?

Five more minutes, he thought. *Five more minutes and I'll start searching for them.* He couldn't stall much longer. And the others could definitely sense that something was awry. They weren't blind. Those two unoccupied folding chairs were so damn conspicuous. . . .

Maybe the partnership idea had backfired. Maybe Linda and Julia had rebelled against his authority and fled. But no, that was impossible. Linda had conceived the whole partnership plan in the first place. *She* was the one who wanted to keep an eye on Julia, to help the Healer turn her against George—

The barn door flew open.

Harold's head jerked up. *Finally!*

Linda staggered inside, practically dragging Julia behind her. What had *happened* to them? They looked like war refugees—their robes soiled, their hair in wild disarray.

"Where have you *been?*" he shouted. "Why have you—"

He broke off in midquestion. Julia was crying. Her soft, elfin face was damp and swollen. Her eyes were so puffy, she could barely open them. He took a step toward her.

"Julia's in trouble," Linda whispered gravely.

Harold swallowed. "What kind of trouble?"

"Her ex-boyfriend showed up here this morning," Linda stated. "The last time he saw her, he threatened to kill her. Julia's scared out of her mind. She's afraid to show her face—"

"Why didn't you come to me earlier?" Harold interrupted. His tone was gentle. "I would have taken care of this."

"I *couldn't!*" Julia wailed. Her voice was so hoarse, he could hardly recognize it. "I'm scared of . . ." The rest of her words were lost in sobs.

"I forced her to come here," Linda murmured. She gently stroked Julia's brown curls. "I knew you would put an end to it."

Harold nodded. He suddenly found that he was consumed with rage at this boy he'd never met— this lowlife scum who had reduced such a beautiful girl to a shambling wreck of a human being. It wasn't *right*. Julia didn't even look like herself. Her pristine features were marred by exhaustion and fear and sadness. No, this wouldn't do at all. Whoever the fool was, he would pay. He would rue the day he'd ever stumbled upon the Promised Land.

"What am I going to do?" Julia whispered.

"You're going to sit down and relax," Harold soothed. "Your worries are over. I'm here to protect you. To heal you. You're going—"

"Oh, my *God!*" Julia shrieked.

Harold flinched. *What the hell?*

Julia wrenched herself free from Linda and flung an arm toward the door. Her bloodshot eyes bulged.

75

She stumbled backward, nearly tripping over her own feet. "No, no, no . . ."

Scowling, Harold followed Julia's outstretched finger.

A tall, filthy, malnourished boy stood just inside the barn door.

Harold cringed. The boy obviously hadn't eaten a substantial meal in weeks. His pale skin looked as if it were pulled tightly over the bones of his face. His sunken blue eyes were glazed; his tattered clothing appeared to be several sizes too large. Harold glanced back at Julia. She was huddled behind Linda, gaping at the poor wretch in terror. She was actually *shivering*.

Harold's brow grew furrowed. He couldn't believe it. *This* was the boyfriend? For a split second he was almost tempted to laugh. He'd been expecting some hulking, macho, athletic type—not somebody who looked like a famine victim. Harold could probably snap any one of those pencil-thin bones with his bare hands.

"Julia?" the boy croaked. His eyes narrowed. He leaned forward—and nearly tipped over. He grabbed the door frame for support. "Jeez . . . is that *you?*"

She didn't answer. A strange mewling passed her lips. The noise didn't even sound human. It sounded more like the last whine of a fatally wounded animal.

That's enough.

Harold planted himself squarely in front of the boy, blocking his line of sight. "What's your name?" he barked.

"Luke," the boy muttered. He craned his skinny neck. "I know that girl—"

"I know," Harold growled. "You threatened to kill her."

Luke froze, gaping at him. He shook his head. "No, no," he whispered. "I love her."

"Liar!" Julia shouted. "You're a dirty *liar!*"

Harold folded his arms across his chest. "Looks like she doesn't believe you, Luke," he stated. "And neither do I. You're not welcome here. I don't allow liars in the Promised Land."

"But you—you gotta under-understand," he stammered. He coughed once. "I'm not the same person I was. I've been through hell. I swear to you—"

"How convenient," Harold interrupted. His tone was flat. "You've had a change of heart. Now I suppose you're a saint, right?"

Luke shook his head again, clutching the door frame as if it were a life raft. "Just listen to me," he pleaded. His voice cracked. His eyes were watering. "I don't want any trouble. I've had enough trouble. I was beaten and left for dead. I just need to find the Healer, okay?"

Harold raised his eyebrows. "You found him. And he wants you to leave."

"You?" Luke wheezed. His face whitened. "But I . . . I . . ."

"What do you *want?*" Harold demanded. Despite his annoyance and anger, he was strangely fascinated by this boy. Judging from Julia's obvious panic, Luke must have once possessed a terrible, intimidating strength. What could have possibly happened to reduce him to this pitiful state—other than mere starvation?

"I want you to heal me," Luke whispered tremblingly. He closed his eyes. His body began to shake with silent, convulsive sobs. "I know you can cure the plague. I came so far to find you. So far. You don't understand. Please. I'm running out of time." He took a deep breath. "Just help me. Help me and I swear I'll do anything—"

"Don't listen to him!" Julia yelled. "Let him die. He turned twenty-one last month. It'll happen any day. He *deserves* it. He deserves worse. I know how that sounds . . . I'd never say that about anyone else. Just him. Go on and let him die."

It's not like I have a choice in the matter, Harold thought, but he smiled at Luke as if he did—as if the fate of Luke's existence rested in the palm of his hand. Because in spite of Harold's awesome abilities, despite the miracles, despite the *rumors* . . . there was one power that still eluded him. And that was the most important power of all.

It was the power to cure the plague.

Of course, he'd never *tried* to cure it. He didn't even know where to begin. The truth of the matter was that he tried not to think about the plague at all. His own birthday was rapidly approaching. . . .

But Luke didn't need to know any of that. No. Luke needed to *squirm*, to suffer as he'd made Julia suffer.

"Oh, God," Luke whispered. He sank to the floor and rested his head between his bony knees. "Oh, God."

"You brought this on yourself, Luke," Julia stated tonelessly. "Don't blame me."

Harold smirked.

Luke slowly lifted his dull, waterlogged eyes. "Julia . . . Julia, I don't blame you for hating me." He swallowed. "I don't. I just—I want you to know that I'm sorry. I'm sorry for the way I treated you. But I did it . . . I did it 'cause I loved you. I always did. Okay?"

Oh, please, Harold thought.

Nobody said a word.

"Wait a minute!" Linda cried.

Harold frowned, glancing over his shoulder.

Linda took one step away from Julia. Her eyes widened, flashing between Luke and Harold. Then she gasped. She looked stricken.

"What is it?" Harold demanded.

"I've seen this before," Linda murmured. She sounded as if she were talking to herself. "In a vision. I've seen all of this. *Exactly.*" She nodded at Harold. "You're going to save this boy's life. I've seen it. It's going to be your greatest miracle. Your greatest!"

A hushed, bewildered murmur rose from the circle of Visionaries.

Save him? Harold shot a hard glance at Julia. She was shaking her head, horrified. His heart rate increased slightly. Saving Luke was impossible. Unless . . .

"Please!" Luke screamed. *"Now!"*

Harold spun back toward the door. *Uh-oh.* Luke's face was turning bright red. He lunged forward and fell to his hands and knees, fighting to crawl toward Harold—and a hideous black welt bubbled across his arm.

"Heal him!" Linda cried.

Before Harold could move, she dashed in front of him and swept Luke's liquefying body into her arms. Harold cringed. The passing seconds seemed to slow to an excruciating plod. Terror and doubt closed in on him. Was this *real?* Was the power now truly *his?* Linda's visions had never been wrong before. . . .

"Lay your hands on his head!" Linda commanded, thrusting the limp heap of flesh toward him. Luke's face was already covered in frothy black blisters. "Do it!"

What if I fail? What if—

Holding his breath, Harold reached out with his right hand and placed the tips of his fingers on the top of Luke's greasy scalp.

The bubbling ceased.

The barn froze.

If anyone was breathing, Harold didn't hear it. Not a sound. His eyes roved over Luke's body—very meticulously, inch by inch. He felt as if he were examining a single frame of film on a long reel. As far as he could tell, the plague was caught in a state of suspended animation. Luke wasn't melting. The blisters remained; blood dripped from open sores . . . but he was alive. He was solid. He was *whole.*

My greatest miracle.

"You did it," Luke gasped. A shaky smile spread across his cracked lips. "You *did* it!"

Harold's heart broke into a savage, hammering thump. For a moment he thought he might faint. He still couldn't grasp the implications of what had just happened. For the first time in his life, he didn't feel like the genius he knew himself to be. His mind was in a stupor.

My greatest miracle.

"The Chosen One," Linda whispered.

He blinked a few times.

Slowly, very slowly . . . the realization dawned on him. Euphoria spread through his body in delicious ripples. Before he knew it, Linda had thrown her arms around his neck.

"I love you!" she cried. "I love you!"

Well. *That* got the old synapses firing again. The feel of that lithe female form pressed against his skin was just what he needed. Yes, yes. He glanced at Luke and started laughing. The boy was alive. *Alive.* It was so fitting, wasn't it? It was fitting that this miracle represented the pinnacle of Harold's triumph. He had always wanted to save lives, to be a real doctor. It was his greatest wish, his life's passion, his one dream . . . ever since he was a child.

And now he was the *only* doctor. With a capital *D.* Luke was his diploma, his certificate of authenticity.

Yes, Harold Wurf had *cured* the plague. Cured it! With the mystical touch of his divine hand, he'd cast the evil out of this boy's body. There was hope for everyone in the Promised Land. His flock would live forever. He could truly heal them, *all* of them, every single one. . . .

My greatest miracle.

The ecstasy of the moment consumed him totally.

"I am the Healer!" he shouted with raucous abandon. "I *am* the Chosen One!"

187 Puget Drive,
Babylon, Washington
June 9–16

June 9

What's that old saying? "The more
things change, the more things stay the
same." Something like that. Anyway, that
choice little line pretty much sums up
my life these days.

For one thing, I'm back to being the
hostess with the mostest. Everybody
wants to hang with me and my best
friend. Just like old times.

The only difference is that I traded
in my old best friend for one that I
actually _like_.

Pretty wild, huh? Everybody loves
Leslie. It's weird, too, because I used to
get really jealous when people paid more

attention to Jezebel than me. But with Leslie, I have no trouble sharing the spotlight. I don't even know why. We started on such a sour note. Not to mention the fact that I _am_ catty and kind of a bitch.

We just complement each other in a way I can't explain. We have nothing in common. She's a nondrinker; her sense of style sucks; she's kind of bubbly . . . but she cracks me up. It's like she's yin and I'm yang. (Jeez. I sound like a self-help video.)

The best part of it is that she's totally rallying everybody against Trevor. I get such a kick out of watching her. Since she doesn't drink, she hangs a lot with the COFs. (Pronounced "coughs"—our newest, private little term for the Chosen One freaks. Get it? Ha, ha, ha.)

It's amazing how much she's mellowed them out. She's all, like: "Don't you think the Chosen One would want people to get along? Don't you think the Chosen One would want you to love thy neighbor?" And it works. I have to give her props. She is a BS artist of the highest degree.

Of course, it probably helps that every single male slobbers like a dog when she's around.

Did I mention how much I love Caleb? The guy is such a sweetie. He never ceases to outdo himself. Here I am, totally bumming that I have no M&M's, and Caleb spends all day tracking some down. Most of the stores in Babylon are cleaned out, so he went all the way to Ogdenville. On <u>foot.</u> It's probably fifteen miles away.

He said something half jokingly that made me sort of sad, though. After we scarfed down all the M&M's, Caleb was like: "I knew I had to bribe you to spend time with me." He was laughing, but I could tell he was sort of serious, too. It's obvious he thinks that I don't pay as much attention to him as I used to, now that I'm back home. And I guess I _am_ being kind of a social butterfly. Most of my days are spent hanging out with Leslie, watching her talk trash about my brother.

But what can I do? It's for a good cause. As soon as there are enough kids around here and everyone is psyched, Leslie is going to take down W.I. She's totally fired up for it. I think she'll be able to do it, too. Then our problems will be solved. We'll have food and electricity and God knows what else Trevor has stashed away.

And when _that_ happens, I'll be able to spend every single second with Caleb.

How many seconds are in three years and two months? Not a whole lot. Anyway, that's how much time I have left. I should ask Trevor. He was always good at word problems.

On second thought, I'll just let Leslie kick his ass instead.

Maybe I've been wrong all along. Maybe there _is_ a Chosen One.

I mean it. I actually have to write this down because I think I might be going insane. I'm not joking. Today was really, really freaky.

First of all, this huge swarm of kids shows up on my street. There must have been over a hundred of them, at least. I'm not exaggerating at all. And all of them were COs. _All_ of them. They were from all over the place, too. I heard one of them say he came from Chicago to get here. _Here_. Not anywhere else. Babylon.

That got me thinking. Back in February, we met these COs in Seattle who talked about going to a little town up north. Then I _saw_ one of them. Right out on my front lawn. Just, like, an

87

hour ago. I'm sure it was one of the same kids. No doubt. I'm one hundred percent positive. So I went up to him and asked, "Were you ever in the Citicorp Building in Seattle?" He gave me this really nasty look. It was creepy as hell. It was like he <u>hated</u> me. He told me he wasn't going to waste any time talking to nonbelievers.

Then he melted. Poof. One second he's dissing me; the next second he's turning into black goo. I've been hiding out in my bedroom ever since.

June 13

I just remembered something. Brian's birthday was last week. He turned twenty-one. So I better stop writing because now I think I might cry and that's really lame because I'm just going to get the paper all smudgy and that won't be any good and

Hang on, Bri. We're going to be there soon. I swear, okay?

Today was the worst day of my entire seventeen-year existence. Even rotting away in Trevor's cell was better. I'm serious.

It started this morning. Out of nowhere, Jezebel comes waltzing back into my life. Unannounced. And <u>definitely</u> unwanted. Apparently she broke out of WAS because she was bored or something, and now she wants to hang out with me again. She wants to pick up where we left off New Year's Eve. She actually said that.

That means she wants to conveniently forget about all the stuff that happened in between. Like blowing me off for Trevor. Like leaving me and Brian and Jack to die in the freezing rain. I can't believe that I even <u>thought</u> about forgiving her or patching things up. Just seeing her again made me want to yack. Literally.

So I was honest. I told her that she better get lost, or I might spew barf on her precious black shirt. What can I say? I've never been good at hiding my feelings. I told her that I had a real friend now. (Oh, yeah—one funny thing did happen. When Jez first came walking up, Leslie whispered to me: "Who's the vampire with a day pass?" I couldn't have summed up Jez's cheesy goth-rocker look better myself.)

Then Jez told me that Brian died.

Maybe she said it to make me mad. I don't know. But I can always tell when she's lying. She gets really fidgety and blinks a lot and tugs at that dyed black hair.

This time she didn't do any of that stuff. Nothing. So I guess Brian really is dead. And he died thinking that I hated him.

To top things off, just to make the whole day perfect, Caleb and I got into our first official fight as a couple. He asked me why I was bawling my eyes out, and I told him it was because my ex-boyfriend died. There was no reason to lie. It's not like I still wanted to have passionate sex with Brian or anything. I just felt bad about the way things turned out. Brian was still my friend. He'll <u>always</u> be my friend.

But Caleb just didn't get it. And that made me even more sad because usually he gets everything. So instead of comforting me, he stormed off.

Why is my life falling apart?

In all of this craziness, though, there <u>is</u> one good thing. After all, I have to remember that I <u>am</u> Miz Positivity. Happy, happy, happy.

The good thing is that Jezebel got out so easily.

Not that she's <u>here</u>, obviously. It's just that it's a good sign that she left WIS at all. It makes me think that Trevor is slipping. Because I know for a fact that Trevor would never, ever let her go. He's totally horny for her. And he's scared of her, too. He thinks she has all these wicked, gnarly powers. We're talking _Jezebel_. What a laugh! The only power she has is the power to make me ill.

Anyway, I think Leslie will make her move soon. Then we'll have all the amenities of WAS, and Caleb and I will make up, and life will be peachy again.

Right?

ELEVEN

**Amarillo,
Texas
Afternoon of June 19**

There is no moon. The night is black.

I can almost see the Demon.

She looks like one of us—like a person. Like a girl. Like the Chosen One. But she has no face, no eyes, no features I can see in the darkness. I just know she's there.

I know that she's frightened of my baby.

That's why she won't come any closer. My baby holds part of the key. Not all of it, but part of it. And as I stare down into those beautiful eyes—one green and one brown—I know that I have to find out soon. Time is running out. I can feel it slipping away.

The Demon is laughing now, but the laughter is empty. She's scared. . . .

George Porter opened his eyes.

He sat up straight on the damp, rough concrete and brushed his stringy blond hair out of his face. Then he scowled.

Crap. Why did I wake up?

Funny. He used to be scared of his visions. He

93

used to freak out whenever he felt one coming on. Now he actually found himself looking forward to them. Yup. He was bummed when they were over. Because as sick as it seemed, those flashes let him escape. They were the only thing that kept him from losing it in this hellhole.

At least I'm having them more often.

He hopped to his feet and wiped the moist seat of his grimy black jeans. His butt hurt. He squinted toward the locked door. When was he going to be fed? Was it dinnertime yet? The worst thing about being stuck here was that he could never tell *what* time it was. Harold's cellar was always dark. There were no windows. There was *nothing.* Not even a blanket. Just dripping stone walls and rusted pipes and a stinking hole for a toilet.

Well, that was *something,* he supposed. When he'd been locked down with Eight Ball in the Pittsburgh city joint, there were no bathroom facilities at all. He'd been forced to do his business on the floor.

Yeah . . . recently he'd been thinking a lot about those days in jail. He'd been thinking mostly about how Eight Ball wouldn't shut up. Eight Ball kept going on about how they were in hell, that being in hell meant being trapped together forever. But now George knew that he was wrong. Being *alone* was a whole lot worse than being trapped with another person—even a fat *putz* like Eight Ball.

Because when you were by yourself and you had only your own thoughts to keep you company, you could get deep into your own brain . . . *way* deep, and there was stuff down in there that was bad and dark and scary. It only came out when everything else was gone—

"I'm going crazy," he said out loud.

The last syllable echoed briefly off the bare walls: *"zee . . . zee . . ."*

Fear scuttled at the edges of his mind. He *was* going crazy, wasn't he? Every few minutes or so he'd feel a sudden jab, a *tick*. It made him jump. He was sure that an invisible hand was swatting him on the back of the neck, pushing him to bust out of here and hightail it west as fast as he could. It kept getting worse, too. It *stung*. And when he wasn't fighting to ignore that or reminiscing about jail, he was thinking about Julia. He'd make up whole conversations in his head. He'd imagine talking to her for hours and hours on end, just picturing her soft brown eyes. . . .

Stop! His breathing quickened. He glanced at the door again. It was just wood—damp, old wood. It wasn't a metal vault or anything. It was probably pretty flimsy, as a matter of fact.

He bit his lip.

"Let me outta here!"

The words shot out of his gut like a cannon, burning his dry throat, flooding the room with sound. He didn't even know they were coming. But there was no controlling himself now. He didn't *want* to control himself. Sucking in his breath, he threw himself across the room and hurled his body against the door.

"Ow!"

A stinging pain shot through his elbow. But nothing else happened. The door hardly even rattled. He stood there, grimacing and rubbing his aching bone, feeling more pathetic and helpless than he ever had in his whole freaking life.

All right. It didn't matter. He could hold out. He could stay down in this basement for another month if he had to. He'd been born and raised on the mean streets of Pittsburgh. Suffering was nothing new to him. It only made him stronger. Nothing could ever make him believe that Harold was the Chosen One— just like nothing could ever stop him from loving Julia.

Nothing.

And then the lock clicked.

George froze. His eyes narrowed. The knob was turning. . . .

The door flew open, nearly knocking him over.

It was Harold, of course. Who else? He stood in the doorway at the bottom of the steps and flashed George that slick con man's smile—the way he always did. He was still wearing that same stupid white lab coat. Didn't he realize that it made him look like an idiot?

"You want to get out?" Harold asked.

George scowled. "What the hell do *you* think? I'm not screaming and banging on this door for my health."

"Do you even remember why I put you here?"

George started rubbing his elbow again. "I try not to think about it," he muttered.

Harold sighed. "Let me refresh your memory, then. I put you here because you violated my commandments."

George glared at him. It figured that Harold was still clinging to that lame-ass lie. Maybe he thought that George would start to believe it if he heard it enough times. "Is there a point to this? You're boring me."

"Always the rebel, aren't you?" Harold smirked. "Yes, there is a point to this. I want you to join the ranks of the Promised Land again. I want you to be reunited with Julia. I want to *save* you."

"Don't mess with my head, Harold," George growled. "I'm not in the mood for playing."

Harold shrugged. "This isn't a game. The choice rests with you."

"Fine," George spat. "You're gonna let me out. Right on. So what do I gotta do?"

Once again Harold flashed that used-car-salesman smile. "I want you to talk to somebody. A friend of mine. I believe you two have already met." He glanced over his shoulder and stepped aside.

A lone figure in a white robe lumbered slowly down the steps.

George's eyes bulged. His face wrinkled in disgust.

It was that dude *Luke*. Julia's old boyfriend. The one who'd tried to get him snuffed out in Ohio. Here. How the hell . . . Or maybe it wasn't Luke because this guy sure looked a lot different. He looked like death. For one thing, he'd lost about forty pounds. And he must have caught some kind of terrible disease because his pasty white face was covered with quarter-size black scabs.

"Luke?" George asked. He felt like retching—or throwing a punch. "Is that *you?*"

Luke nodded blankly.

"What *happened* to you?"

"The Healer saved me," he answered. "He cast out the plague."

George took a step back. *Whoa.* This was too weird. Seeing Luke was strange enough, but something sick had happened to him. He didn't *sound* saved. He sounded like one of those computerized phone menus: polite, mechanical, and totally flat.

"What do you mean?" George gasped.

"He means I healed him," Harold said sharply. "I laid my hands on him and cast out the plague at the very moment it was killing him."

George's eyes flashed back to Luke.

"It's true," Luke whispered.

No way. George didn't know what kind of stunt Harold was trying to pull by bringing Luke here—but there was no way in hell that he "cast out the plague." George might be going crazy, but he wasn't gullible. Nope. Harold had probably starved Luke and burned him repeatedly with a cigar or cattle prod, then drugged him with some downers. Or maybe they were both in on it together. Yeah. Maybe they were part of some huge conspiracy with those girls from Ohio. Why else would Luke be in Texas? *That* was an explanation George would buy.

"What's the matter, George?" Harold asked.

"Nothing," George mumbled. "You were talking about letting me out?"

Harold grinned. "That's right. I brought Luke down here because I want the two of you to work together. I want you to be partners. Luke will help you understand who I am and what I can do for you. But you have to accept me as the Chosen One. It's your only choice."

Partners with Luke? George would rather eat his own barf. But he kept his mouth shut.

"Luke's beautiful former girlfriend has already accepted me," Harold went on. "Remember Julia? *She* knows I can cure the plague. And I've promised to return you to her once you've accepted that. I never break my promises."

George's blood simmered. Harold loved torturing him with the fact that Julia had somehow fallen for that bull. But she'd see the truth sooner or later. George just had to talk to her, to *see* her . . . to hold her. His visions were getting stronger. That meant *her* visions must be getting stronger, too. As long as he could put on an act long enough to get out of here, then things would be cool. The two of them could leave this place. Together.

"What do you have to say to that?" Harold asked.

"Okay, you got me," George lied, hanging his head. "I'm ready to be partners—"

A door slammed upstairs.

Harold and Luke both glanced over their shoulders.

"Healer?" a girl's high-pitched voice cried. "Healer?"

"Down here, Linda," Harold answered.

Linda? George clenched his fists at his side as she clattered down the steps. *Damn.* It figured that bitch would show up right when he was on the verge of getting out of here. She'd screw everything up for him. *She* was the one who'd gotten George into this mess in the first place. She was in on the conspiracy, too. . . .

"I had a vision," Linda gasped breathlessly. Her cheeks were bright red. "Just now. A terrible, terrible vision."

George groaned. *Gimme a goddamn break.*

"What was it?" Harold asked.

Linda shook her head. "I saw another plague descending on the Promised Land." She spoke quickly. "The worst yet. It was a punishment for a traitor. Somebody's going to lie to you and betray you." She lifted a finger at George. "And I saw George's face. He's tricking you right now—"

"That's *crap!*" George snarled. "You're lying! You're setting me up right now—"

"Shut up," Harold snapped. He whirled back to face George. "I should have known. You really thought you could fool me, didn't you?"

George held out his hands. "No. Look, man, you gotta let me out of here—"

"Don't listen to him," Linda warned.

"I won't," Harold stated. "Believe me. Julia was counting on you to see the light of truth. It looks like I'll have to disappoint her. What a waste." He glanced at Linda and Luke. "We're done here. Let's go."

"No, no," George protested. His stomach plummeted.

The three of them shuffled out the door. He took a step forward. "Hey—"

The door slammed shut. Three pairs of footsteps vanished up the stairs.

"Hey!" George shouted again.

Once again the room was silent, bathed in near total blackness.

And at that moment George realized something. It struck him with a certainty he'd never experienced before in his whole life. *I'll never make it out of this cellar alive.*

PART III

June 21–30

TWELVE

Jefferson Municipal Park,
Akron, Pennsylvania
Afternoon of June 21

"Hey, Sarah? Sarah, are you awake?"

Sarah grunted. She wouldn't open her eyes. She *was* awake, but not by choice. She wanted to sleep, desperately, but her exhausted body ached too much—not to mention that it was almost impossible to get comfortable on such a narrow park bench. What did Aviva want, anyway? Wasn't *she* just as tired and run down as Sarah was?

"I found some kids," Aviva whispered excitedly. "We might even be able to get something to eat."

Something to eat? Sarah supposed she was hungry. The last item of solid food to cross her lips was a very old doughnut, sometime last night. But the rumblings in her stomach were far less painful than the throbbing in her hips or the burning in her feet. Couldn't Aviva wait just a *little* while longer? They were supposed to rest today. For a full day. That was the agreement. Until now they'd only stopped at night. Every single hour of daylight was spent marching westward. They must have covered five hundred miles in two weeks,

105

over cracked roads and highways that all blended into one. . . .

"You told me to come get you if I ran into any kids," Aviva reminded her.

"I know, I know," Sarah grumbled. She forced herself to open her eyelids.

Her lips immediately twisted into a frown. Maybe she *had* fallen asleep. The sky was completely overcast. A breeze was blowing. It was almost chilly. But the sun had been blazing when she had first collapsed on this bench.

"Are you okay?" Aviva asked.

Sarah nodded and sat up straight, rubbing her bare arms. "I'm fine," she muttered. "It just . . . uh, it looks like it might storm."

Aviva nodded. "Yeah," she said vaguely. "The temperature has really dropped, too." She wrapped her arms around herself, shivering in her ratty sundress.

She needs some new clothes, Sarah thought sadly. Aviva's dress was falling apart. The poor girl hadn't changed *once* since Sarah had met her—almost three months ago. She didn't have a choice, of course. Everything she owned had been lost or destroyed in the March flood. Then again, Sarah herself hadn't changed in over three weeks. She still wore the same T-shirt and jeans she'd been wearing when she fell overboard. . . .

"What's wrong?" Aviva murmured.

"Nothing," Sarah lied. But she was thinking: *We've come all the way to Pennsylvania, and we haven't seen anyone else until now. That means only*

*one thing. It's obvious. Lilith and her "servants" have
gotten rid of every single kid between here and New
York. They're all dead.*

She suddenly felt as if a heavy veil had been
draped over her head, blocking out every color
and reducing the world to a dismal black and
white. How could she possibly expect to triumph
over Lilith? Here she was, sitting in a weed-
choked park, under a cloudy sky, in a strange city,
lost and alone. . . .

"Well, anyway, I found a whole bunch of kids,"
Aviva went on. "They seemed to be having fun, too. I
mean, I didn't talk to any of them—but they're hanging out in a video arcade. I guess there wasn't a
blackout here, like there was in New York. It's just
down the block."

"Sounds good," Sarah said absently.

"Hey, Sarah, can I ask you something?"

She shrugged. "Sure."

"How come you didn't tell Darrell the truth?"

Darrell? She cast Aviva a sharp glance. "What do
you mean?"

Aviva lowered her eyes. "I just . . . how come you
didn't tell him you were the Chosen One?" Her voice
was so quiet that Sarah could barely hear it over the
wind. "He probably would have come with us if he
knew. He probably could have convinced everyone
else on that bridge to come, too. You would have had
followers again."

Sarah swallowed. Why? There were a hundred
reasons.

No. She was lying to herself. And she knew it. She

hadn't told Darrell she was the Chosen One because he wouldn't believe her. It was *that* simple. He would think she was crazy. How could she possibly prove it without the scroll?

"Are you afraid of telling people?" Aviva whispered.

Something like that, Sarah thought.

"You're worried that people will vaporize if they deny you," Aviva said gravely. "Just like what happened to that boy on the boat. You don't want people to die, so you're keeping it a secret. That's it, isn't it? You're afraid of your own powers."

Sarah stared back at her. *My God.* She'd completely forgotten about that boy—the one who had melted right in front of her after accusing her of being a fake. It had even been written in the scroll: "Those who deny . . . will surely perish." Or something like that. The point was that Aviva was right. Sarah *could* prove she was the Chosen One. She didn't want anyone to have to die . . . but on the other hand, she couldn't continue with only *one* follower. If she were going to have any chance at all against Lilith, she needed *numbers.*

"It's time to start spreading the word about who you really are," Aviva stated. "The more people who know, the better off we'll be. Even if a few kids die, it'll be worth it in the end. I know that sounds terrible, but it's true." Her voice dropped. "See, when you were asleep, I had another vision."

Sarah swallowed. "You did?"

Aviva nodded. "I saw somebody who's pretending to be the Chosen One. A *boy.* A false prophet.

Lilith is helping him, and he doesn't even know it. We're getting close to him, and we need people to stop him—"

"Hold on," Sarah interrupted. "Did you say . . . false prophet?"

Aviva nodded.

Wait a second. Sarah's eyes narrowed. Wasn't a false prophet mentioned in the scroll? *Yes.* Some of the prophecies concerned a phony miracle worker. And he was supposed to be in the "New World." America, obviously. Aviva's visions were right on the mark. Sarah forced herself to stand on her sore legs. This was important. Her entire body twinged for a moment, but she ignored the pain. It was time for action.

"Let's go check out that arcade," she said.

Once again she felt that same vigor, that same *purpose* she'd felt at the Empire State Building. She followed Aviva down a gravel path that led out to a broad, deserted avenue. One side was lined with a squat strip mall: a barbershop, a copying center, a video store . . . all abandoned. Sarah glanced at the gray sky again. The day had grown so dark that the streetlights were on—flickering with a pale fluorescence. Strange. Now that she thought about it, the *presence* of electricity was almost more odd than the absence of it. Working traffic lights and neon advertising signs seemed entirely out of place in a ghost town.

"This is it," Aviva announced. She halted in front of a darkly tinted glass door.

Before Sarah could even reply, Aviva pulled it

open—unleashing a bombardment of blue flashes, bells, alarms, whistles . . . and chattering kids. *Lots* of kids.

Sarah gasped. *Wow*. Walking into this place was like entering a time machine. People were actually *laughing* in here. Sarah blinked a few times, shaking her head. It was as if the plague had never happened.

"Pretty incredible, huh?" Aviva whispered, closing the door behind them. "I think there's a big popcorn maker around here somewhere. . . ."

Sarah laughed out loud. Even the *smell* in this place was like something out of the past. It reeked of spilled junk food and sweaty bodies.

"So what do you want to do?" Aviva asked, raising her voice to be heard over the din.

"I'm not sure." Sarah surveyed the crowd. Nobody seemed to notice that they were there. Every kid was hunched over a video game—wrestling with plastic guns or joysticks and slapping buttons. "You think I should just introduce myself? You think I should just tell people who I am and see what happens?"

"Yeah." Aviva nodded toward two boys. "Why don't you start with those guys?"

Sarah hesitated. *Those guys?* Both were hipster, druggie types: backward baseball caps, pierced ears, and baggy jeans that looked as if they could fit about five people at once. One kid was about a foot taller than the other. The short one was playing a game in a frenzy, jerking spastically. They looked like trouble. But she took a deep breath and marched over to them. If she'd learned anything from Darrell, it was that she couldn't judge people by their appearances. Besides, the *truth* was on her side. It wouldn't fail her. It never had.

"Hi," she said.

The short one glanced at her out of the corner of his eye as he played. "What's up?" he asked. His tone was casual, as if he'd known her all his life. "Wanna play doubles?"

"Um . . . no thanks," she mumbled, trying to smile. "I actually have something important to tell you."

He nodded distractedly. "Yeah, yeah, I know. You think I look like Tom Cruise. Don't worry. It happens all the time."

She smirked. "Actually, no. This has nothing to do with you. It has to do with me."

He shot her another confused glance.

All of a sudden the machine beeped loudly, and a sad little melody burst from the speakers. The words *Game Over* flashed across the screen.

"Dammit!" He slapped the console and rolled his eyes at his friend. "I was, like, a thousand points from the high score." He turned to her, then grinned. "Look what you made me do. This better be important."

Sarah tried to smile again. But she was starting to feel extremely nervous. Was this really such a good idea? Did she really plan on going around to every single kid in here and simply announcing that she was the Chosen One? And what would happen if they denied her? Would they really melt right in front of her eyes?

"Well?" he asked, raising his eyebrows.

"Have you . . . have you ever heard of the Chosen One?" she stammered awkwardly.

He exchanged a quick look with the tall one. "Sure. He's in the back. He's playing Super Mario Brothers."

Sarah swallowed. "No, you don't understand," she whispered. *"I'm* the Chosen One."

The short one nodded. His expression remained blank. "Sure, you are. And I'm the reincarnation of Madonna. Her spirit passed into my body when she caught the plague."

"Yeah," his friend chimed in. "I'm the entire cast of *Friends*. I got six glamorous Hollywood personalities for the price of one."

Sarah pursed her lips. Great. So they were comedians. "I'm not joking," she grumbled.

"And I'm not laughing," the short one said. "So what's the problem?"

The tall one chuckled.

Jerks. Sarah's cheeks felt hot. But she kept her mouth clamped tightly shut. They wouldn't be laughing for long. Soon their flesh would begin to bubble and everyone in here would see—

"Sarah!" Aviva's shrill voice tore across the room. "Sarah, it's snowing!"

What? Sarah spun around. Her eyes widened. Aviva was right. The sky outside the windows was a charcoal gray. Huge white flakes tumbled to the earth. The trees across the street were already sprinkled with a frosty layer of white. But how could it possibly be *snowing?* It was June. It was the first day of summer. Unless . . .

This is the sign! This is the miracle that always happens when people doubt me!

Sarah whirled back around to face the boys. "See that!" she cried. "That snow *proves* I'm the Chosen One. Why else would it snow right now?"

The short one cocked an eyebrow. "Uh . . . maybe for the same reason we were overrun by grasshoppers last month? I didn't see you around then."

"And how about that flood in the spring?" the tall one asked. "Did you wave your magic wand for that one, too?"

Sarah shook her head. This was crazy. They *still* didn't believe her.

"Look," the short one stated flatly. "Everybody who believes in that garbage has already split for Texas. People are actually dumb enough to think that some guy down there can cure the plague. So if you think you can prove them all wrong, go find him. But right now, you're talking to the wrong guys. 'Cause we don't give a crap."

"That must be him!" Aviva cut in excitedly. "The guy in Texas—that's the False Prophet!"

Of course. Sarah's mood suddenly lifted. It would make perfect sense. And if that guy *were* the False Prophet—and Sarah found him—then she would be that much closer to finding Lilith. After all, Lilith was supposed to be helping him. And even if she *didn't* find Lilith, Sara could still gain followers by exposing the False Prophet for the fraud he was.

"The 'False Prophet'?" the short boy asked disdainfully.

Sarah glowered at him. *Time to go*. She'd spent more than enough time in this arcade. "Where in Texas is he?" she demanded.

"Dunno," the guy muttered, turning back to the machine. "Just head south, and I'm sure you'll find him sooner or later."

"Yeah," the tall one added. "In the meantime, why don't you make yourself useful? Go shovel out our front walk."

THIRTEEN

187 Puget Drive,
Babylon, Washington
Night of June 23

Caleb Walker hated it when people were late. *Hated* it. There was nothing more annoying than waiting around for somebody to show up—especially somebody who should have been here *two hours ago*. He could have done anything with that time. He could have slept. He could have curled up with a good book . . . say, for instance, *Skintight: The Illustrated History of Erotic Film*. He could have taught himself basket weaving.

But instead he'd wasted two hours being bored.

It was a crime. There was nothing worse than being bored. Absolutely nothing. With every beer he pounded and pill he popped—and he'd pounded and popped several of each already—he waged a holy war in the name of boredom avoidance. There simply wasn't enough time left for yawning or thumb twiddling anymore.

Where the hell was Ariel?

He pushed himself off the edge of her unmade bed and lumbered over to the window, nearly tripping on the seventies-style purple shag carpeting. *Damn.* Shouldn't she get rid of this rug? Wasn't it a fire hazard or something? At first, he really dug the retro feel of Ariel's room: the magazine cutouts on the walls, the record player her dad had given her—and, of course, the lava lamp. Now it was starting to get on his nerves. The place practically reeked of polyester.

She better have a good excuse, he thought. He frowned at his reflection in the glass. Was she not interested in him anymore? Was that it? No. She was always telling him how much she loved his long bangs and crooked smile and scruffy cheekbones. So why was she doing this to him? They were supposed to be going out. But they were a couple in theory rather than practice. He sure in hell wasn't getting very much action.

Not that action was the be-all and end-all of a relationship. But it helped. A lot.

He pressed his nose against the cold windowpane and cupped his hands around his eyes, scanning the snowy night for any sign of her. Nope. Nothing. All he saw was a blanket of white fluff over the street. *Snow in June.* Pretty damn weird. Then again, after the locusts, why should he be surprised? *Hold on . . .* There was a fresh pair of footprints leading up to the house.

The front door opened and slammed.

Well, it's about freaking time. He shook his head and snatched a half-empty beer off the night table, then slouched back on the bed. Heavy footsteps plodded up the stairs. Okay, he had to admit, he was psyched that the wait was over. But he wasn't going to give her the satisfaction of knowing that. He made sure his face was as sour as possible.

"Don't worry about me," he called sarcastically as she strolled down the hall. "I've been just fine, sitting here on my butt—"

He stopped talking.

It wasn't Ariel at all. It was that weird chick, Jezebel.

What was *she* doing here?

"Hey, Caleb," she said with a smile. She stood in the doorway, holding a fancy-looking dark bottle in her pale hands. "I figured you would be here."

"Where's Ariel?" he asked impatiently. He wasn't in the mood for small talk.

Jezebel shrugged. "She's still at Old Pine Mall."

Great, he thought miserably. *Just great.* So instead of hanging out with his girlfriend, he could hang out with his girlfriend's worst enemy, the town pariah who looked like the missing fifth member of Hole. He took a long sip of beer and cast her a sidelong glance. Well, she wasn't all *that* bad. She was kind of hot, actually—especially in that tight long-sleeved black T-shirt. She had a pretty curvy body. He could do without the dyed-black hair thing, though.

"Mind if I hang out?" she asked.

He lifted his shoulders. "It's a free country."

"Don't worry," she murmured, sitting beside him on the mattress. "Ariel won't be home for a while."

"I *want* her to come home," he grumbled. "I've been waiting for hours."

She smiled again. "I know. I was just thinking . . .

117

it might be awkward if she walked in and found the two of us sitting on her bed."

Caleb frowned. Okay. He'd had several beers. He wasn't exactly at his sharpest. But did this girl have the hots for him? It sure seemed that way. She was definitely sending him *some* kind of vibe.

"What's wrong?" she asked.

He edged away from her. "Why would it be awkward?"

"Oh, I don't know," she replied nonchalantly. "Maybe because she hates my guts."

"So what are you doing here?"

She looked him directly in the eye and began to unscrew the cap on her bottle. "I didn't come to see Ariel. I came to see *you.*"

His pulse picked up a beat. That was it. Any doubts vanished. She was vibing him, all right. In a serious way.

"You don't talk much, do you?" she asked in a teasing voice. "Why did you want to see me?" he demanded. He sat up straight. "We don't even know each other. All I know is that you were a bitch to my girlfriend."

She raised the bottle to her lips. "That's *her* point of view," she muttered. She tilted back her head and guzzled for a few seconds, then took a deep breath and wiped her lips with her sleeve. "Whew," she gasped, giggling. "That's strong stuff."

"You didn't answer my question," he growled. "Why did you come to see me?"

"'Cause I figured you might be bored?" she suggested hopefully.

He laughed. He couldn't help himself. She was *right,* after all. "How come?" he asked, but his tone was softer.

"Well, I know *I* was bored." She moaned. "I was sitting there in the food court, listening to Leslie go on and on to all these kids about how they had to scrounge up knives and hockey sticks and stuff to use against Trevor. And Ariel was just, like, *laughing—*"

"All right, all right," he interrupted. "Did Ariel say when she was going to come home?"

She took another swig. "No," she croaked, wincing. "It looked like she was gonna be there for a while."

Caleb's shoulders slumped. He stared at the beer bottle in his hands. An unsettling queasiness filled his stomach. So Ariel had just forgotten about him. It was that simple. She'd gotten so caught up in hanging out with Leslie that her own boyfriend had slipped her mind. This was really turning out to be a hell of a night, wasn't it?

"It'll never work, you know," Jezebel mumbled.

He glanced at her. "What's that?"

"Leslie's whole plan to attack WIT or whatever." She shook her head. "Trevor's a lot smarter than she is. The whole place is sealed off. He'll think of something that'll get everyone killed. I mean, you've been there." She tipped the bottle at him, sloshing the liquor inside. "You've seen what he can do."

For some strange reason, Caleb found himself getting angry. Maybe it was Jezebel's not so subtle implication that Ariel and her friends were stupid. *"You* managed to get out of there," he said. "How do you explain that?"

She blinked a few times, smiling coquettishly. "Come on, Caleb," she murmured. "You know about me. Don't you? I'm . . . different."

Oh, brother. He sneered. "No. Explain it to me. What's so different about you?"

"I'm not really Jezebel," she said. She sounded very matter-of-fact, as if she were talking about her shoe size. "I'm something that none of you could ever possibly understand."

He raised his eyebrows. "Like a freak, for instance?"

"Oh, Caleb," she whispered. She clucked her tongue disappointedly. "You always make jokes when you're uncomfortable, don't you? But you know I'm not kidding around. And you know I'm right, too."

Caleb opened his mouth, then closed it. She had a point. She *was* different. A couple of gears weren't linking up in her skull. Yup. Back before the plague, she would have been a prime candidate for a mental institution. He stared at her as he slowly drained the rest of his beer, gulping the lukewarm liquid down in a steady beat.

"Kiss me," she suddenly commanded.

He nearly spat all the beer out onto Ariel's bed. *"What?"*

"You heard me." She placed her own bottle on the night table and leaned close to him. "Kiss me."

"Are you nuts?" He tried to squirm away from her,

but she grabbed his upper thigh. He flinched. Damn! It was *sensitive* up there. "What are you drinking, anyways?"

"Peppermint schnapps," she answered dryly. "You want some?"

"No!" he cried. His eyes widened. Her shiny black nails were gently scratching the surface of his jeans. "Hey! That's enough!"

"Why?" she whispered in a husky voice. "Are you scared?"

"Of course—of course I'm not scared," he stammered. "I—I just—"

"Then what's the problem?" she asked. "I mean, here we are, a boy and a girl. Nobody's around. We might as well get our kicks, right? It's not like your girlfriend is giving you any. She's joined at the hip with Leslie."

Before Caleb could answer, she smothered his lips with her own, fervently pressing him down into the rumpled covers.

Jeez! He tried to struggle, eyes open wide, but he couldn't help but kiss her back. It was a reflex. Besides, he was too confused, too shocked, too wasted. And she was too strong. She was having her way with him. She was *violating* him. It was totally bizarre. And kinky. And interesting, in a weird way. . . .

One thing was for sure.

He wasn't bored anymore.

CHAPTER
FOURTEEN

I'm so scared. These past few days I've been living two lives. Two totally separate souls are sharing my body. I have no control over when one soul comes and the other goes. I only know that they can't be there at the same time. Occasionally I even feel like a third person, standing outside myself, watching them take turns with me.

One of them is hopeful. There is no longer a time limit on her life. When the hour of death inevitably comes, the Healer will strike the plague from her body. She even has thoughts of old age. In her daydreams she and George watch their baby grow up to be a

123

woman . . . a woman blessed with a mystical gift of second sight and a powerful spirit. A leader.

How do I know my baby will be a girl? I'm not sure. I just do—maybe for the same reason I know that I must go west at some point to face the Demon.

The other soul is terrified and suspicious and confused. She doesn't believe she'll ever see George again.

These two souls are me.

I can't believe that the Healer saved Luke. How can he punish me by keeping me away from George and let somebody like Luke live? I know Linda had a vision . . . but it's strange. What's going on with her? Since when did she start hating George? I don't feel like I can trust her anymore. I'm worried she told the Healer that I'm pregnant. I'm worried that the Healer is going to deal with me next.

And I'm worried for another reason, too. A secret reason. I stopped having visions four days ago. As soon as the snow started, the visions went away.

I know this terrible blizzard is a bad omen, like the locusts. The Healer says it's snowing because the Demon still has control over people in the Promised Land. By people, he means George. He never mentions George by name, but he doesn't have to. And since I'm not having visions anymore, I can't help but feel as if the Demon might be gaining control over me, too.

I have to talk to George soon. Because in an entirely different way, there really are two separate souls living in my body—mine and my baby's. That means the decisions I make no longer affect just me. I have to think of my unborn child. And George still doesn't know.

Julia glanced up from her weather-beaten notebook—just to make sure nobody was looking over her shoulder. But every white-robed member of the flock appeared to be minding his or her own business: reading by candlelight, knitting, sleeping . . . simply *sitting* in an effort to carve out a personal space for themselves.

The barn was stuffed to the limit. She felt as if she were packed into a giant subway car at rush hour. But everybody acted as if invisible walls existed between themselves and their neighbors. They all knew that their survival depended on cramming into an enclosed space for an indefinite amount of time. Unspoken boundaries meant a lot.

I wonder how long it'll be before somebody goes stir-crazy, she thought. She squirmed on the hard wood floor. She'd been sitting with her legs crossed and her back hunched for hours now. Her bones were starting to creak. *It's already been snowing for four days. Who knows how long it'll last? It rained for four straight weeks in March. Anything is possible. Anything—*

"Still got that same notebook, huh?"

Julia shuddered. *That voice . . .*

She knew it was Luke even before she spun around. He was standing directly behind her. He looked awful. He must have just come in from the snow—shivering in a dripping, oversized down jacket. His dark hair was soaked and plastered to the side of his head.

He tried to smile.

Bastard. She suddenly found she was irate. For all

she knew, he could have been there for five minutes, reading the whole time as she wrote.

"What are you doing?" she barked. She slammed the diary shut.

His hideously scarred face drooped slightly. "I came to tell you something," he whispered in a quivering voice. "Why are you so mad?"

"Because you're reading over my shoulder!" she yelled.

Luke's shifty eyes darted around the room. A few people nearby twitched uncomfortably. But for once in her life, Julia didn't mind causing a scene. No. She wanted everyone here to see for themselves just how much of a sneak, a fake, and a liar Luke really was.

"I swear I wasn't," Luke whispered. He knelt beside her. "I would never—"

"You'd never *what?*" she interrupted. She leaned away from him, her nose shriveling in revulsion. "You'd never read my diary? Luke, you once *stole* my diary and read the whole thing! Then you called *me* underhanded. Or did you forget that?"

He shook his head. "But that was before. That's what I've been trying to tell you, Julia. If you just let me explain." His voice broke. "Okay?"

Typical. Julia sneered. He was fishing for pity, looking to exploit her soft side. Well, he was in for a big surprise. He didn't know what Julia had learned from George: that life required a person to be cold and hard and brutal every once in a while. And that it felt *good.*

"Luke, do you know what a sociopath is?" she asked.

127

"Huh?" He gazed at her blankly.

"It's a person who doesn't have any morals," she snarled. "No, it's not even a real *person*. It's an animal who pretends to be a human being in order to hide the fact that he's lower than dirt." She stabbed a finger into his thin chest, nearly pushing him to the floor. "It's *you.*"

He shook his head again, struggling to keep his balance with his bony arms. The joints cracked loudly. "No," he insisted. "I mean, yeah—that's what I was." He scratched at the scabs on the back of his left hand. "I admit it. But after what happened in February with those girls in Ohio, it was like . . . like I had a revelation or something."

Julia folded her arms across her chest. *More words, more lies,* she thought with disgust. "What *did* happen with those girls, anyway? Did you sleep with all of them and get bored?"

"They tortured me, Julia," he murmured. He sniffed once. "After you escaped, they locked me up and took turns beating me. They wanted to know about your visions. George's too. They're all part of this weird cult. They worship something called Lilith. But when they finally figured out that I couldn't help them, they tossed me out in the middle of a road and left me for dead."

And you deserved it, she finished silently. So Luke discovered that hanging out with a coven of witches wasn't a good idea. Did that mean she was supposed to forgive him for trying to have George killed?

He stared at her for several seconds. Finally he bowed his head. "At first I wondered why I was being punished," he croaked. "And then I remembered all the horrible things I did to you. I wandered around for weeks without food or water or anything . . . just thinking about you and apologizing to you in my mind—"

"Is *that* what you came to tell me?" she cried, cutting him off. "That you thought things over for a while and feel bad? It's . . . I—I can't even listen to this!" Her voice rose to a shriek. "It makes me sick!"

A hush fell over the barn.

Dozens of people were now staring at them. Julia hardly noticed. Her breath came fast. She was grinding her teeth. Her heart pounded. She'd never done anything violent in her life; she'd never even been *tempted* to hurt another living thing, but after all the years he'd beat her and lied to her and cheated on her . . .

"That's not what I came to tell you," he whispered.

Her fingers balled up into two tight fists. "No?" she growled. "What did you come to tell me, then? Spit it out."

He stared at the barn floor and took a deep breath. "I came because I'm worried about George," he said quietly.

"Worried about George?" she repeated, incensed. She laughed once. "How stupid do you think I am?"

"I'm serious." He lifted his gaze. "See, I'm not supposed to tell you, but the Healer assigned me to be George's partner. He wanted me to help George accept him. But then that British girl, Linda, had a vision. So the Healer changed his mind. He's never gonna let George out. Anyway, I heard the Healer and Linda yelling at George back at the house. It

129

sounded bad. I think they're gonna do something to him. So I thought I better warn you. . . ."

No! Hot panic engulfed her. They were going to kill him! It was what she'd known and dreaded and never allowed herself to admit. In an instant she was on her feet and bounding over white-robed bodies, stepping on limbs, tripping and stumbling—sprinting for the barn door.

"Julia, wait!" Luke shouted. "Wait—"

She burst outside and nearly fell on her face.

Good Lord. There must have been at least two feet of snow on the ground. And it kept coming. It was driving so hard, she could barely see. A frigid wind was blowing. The sky was an evil gray, darker than she'd ever seen at any time during the day. She squinted and fought to plow forward, but her feet suddenly felt as if they had been dipped in fire. Of course: She was wearing only a pair of worn, ill-fitting sneakers and a white robe. Her teeth chattered; her body shook violently—but she wrapped her arms around herself and forced herself to trudge the hundred or so yards to the Healer's small, wood frame farmhouse.

By the time she flung open the rickety front door, her hands and feet were numb.

"George!" she shouted hoarsely. "George!"

There was no answer. Her eyes flashed across the front hall: antique mirror, homespun rug, unfinished wood floor, a narrow door. She realized with a mix of apprehension and fear that she'd never actually set foot in the Healer's home before. But there was no time to analyze or doubt. She had to save George.

"George!" she shouted again.

"Julia?" came the Healer's muted, distant reply.

"Where are you?" she cried.

"Don't come down here, Julia," he warned. "Stay up there. . . ."

Her ears honed in on the door. His voice was coming from behind it.

Julia dashed across the hall and threw it open. There was a dark, uneven stone stairwell leading under the house—and Julia plunged down it.

She stopped short when she reached the bottom.

And then she stopped breathing.

The Healer stood with Linda Altman just inside an open doorway into an empty, windowless room. The Healer held a flashlight in one hand. The beam of light was aimed at a heap of clothing on the floor: a leather jacket, a pair of black jeans . . . all stained with a thick black muck.

It can't be. It can't be.

The universe seemed to shrink—folding in on itself until nothing existed except what lay in that circle of light.

"Where is he?" Julia whispered in a dead voice. "Where's George?"

Linda glanced at the Healer, then lowered her eyes.

"He's gone. It's the plague. He melted before we could even break the door down."

Julia shook her head. "No," she breathed. "No. No . . ." She kept repeating the word, holding on to it, *cherishing* it—until it swelled in volume, until it no longer sounded like language . . . until a howling, repetitive, animal cry suffused the grim walls of the Healer's cellar. It was all she had left.

131

The Sixth Lunar Cycle

The Lilum were halfway to victory.

Naamah stood alone in the snowy wasteland that was Harold Wurf's farm, gazing at the starless sky in rapturous delight. It was hard to believe that six months of the Last Year had already passed. Time seemed to flow with ever increasing swiftness. And each passing moment brought Naamah and her sisters another step closer to the glorious New Age. . . .

There was still much work to be done, of course. Naamah had to guard against overconfidence. But Lilith's plans had not only succeeded—they had vastly surpassed expectations. The scroll was either lost in Israel or lying at the bottom of the Red Sea. Nobody would ever crack the code. Very few Seers were left alive. The traps that had been laid around the globe had drawn the Seers to their deaths with surprising ease . . . like moths to brilliant flames.

Some Seers were still needed, obviously. But that

was where the False Prophet served his purpose. Those Seers who had succeeded in crossing the oceans, those who had made it out of New York, those who hadn't already stumbled upon the Final Battleground . . . those were the Seers who flocked to the Promised Land.

And all of them believed in Harold's powers. All of them denied the truth of their visions and accepted Harold as the Chosen One.

Naamah smiled. She couldn't have asked for better timing with that poor fellow Luke. She hadn't even planned to use the antidote on him. But when the opportunity presented itself, it was too good to resist. Every Seer was present. Every one believed that Harold had cured Luke. Even Luke himself believed it. He hadn't noticed that while Naamah was helping him to his feet, she was simultaneously saving him from the plague. . . .

Yes, everything had fallen into place. Harold and his flock were almost ready to begin the march westward. Only one more prophecy needed to be fulfilled.

And soon, very soon, victory would be Lilith's.

COUNTDOWN
to the
MILLENNIUM
Sweepstakes

$2,000 for the year 2000

5...4...3...2...1 MILLENNIUM MADNESS.
The clock is ticking ... enter now to
win the prize of the millennium!

1 GRAND PRIZE:
$2,000 for the year 2000!

2 SECOND PRIZES: $500

3 THIRD PRIZES: balloons, noisemakers,
and other party items (retail value $50)

Official Rules
COUNTDOWN
Consumer Sweepstakes

1. No purchase necessary. Enter by mailing the completed Official Entry Form or print out the official entry form from www.SimonSays.com/countdown or write your name, telephone number, address, and the name of the sweepstakes on a 3" x 5" card and mail it to: Simon & Schuster Children's Publishing Division, Marketing Department, Countdown Sweepstakes, 1230 Avenue of the Americas, New York, New York 10020. One entry per person. Sweepstakes begins November 9, 1998. Entries must be received by December 31, 1999. Not responsible for postage due, late, lost, stolen, damaged, incomplete, not delivered, mutilated, illegible, or misdirected entries, or for typographical errors in the entry form or rules. Entries are void if they are in whole or in part illegible, incomplete, or damaged. Enter as often as you wish, but each entry must be mailed separately.

2. All entries become the property of Simon & Schuster and will not be returned.

3. Winners will be selected at random from all eligible entries received in a drawing to be held on or about January 15, 2000. Winner will be notified by mail. Odds of winning depend on the number of eligible entries received.

4. One Grand Prize: $2,000 U.S. Two Second Prizes: $500 U.S. Three Third Prizes: balloons, noise makers, and other party items (approximate retail value $50 U.S.).

5. Sweepstakes is open to legal residents of U.S. and Canada (excluding Quebec). Winner must be 20 years old or younger as of December 31, 1999. Employees and immediate family

members of employees of Simon & Schuster, its parent, subsidiaries, divisions, and related companies and their respective agencies and agents are ineligible. Prizes will be awarded to the winner's parent or legal guardian if under 18.

6. One prize per person or household. Prizes are not transferable and may not be substituted except by sponsors, in event of prize unavailability, in which case a prize of equal or greater value will be awarded. All prizes will be awarded.

7. All expenses on receipt and use of prize, including federal, state, and local taxes, are the sole responsibility of the winners. Winners may be required to execute and return an Affidavit of Eligibility and Release and all other legal documents that the sweepstakes sponsor may require within 15 days of attempted notification or an alternate winner will be selected.

8. By accepting a prize, a winner grants to Simon & Schuster the right to use his/her name and likeness for any advertising, promotional, trade, or any other purpose without further compensation or permission, except where prohibited by law.

9. If the winner is a Canadian resident, then he/she will be required to answer a time-limited arithmetical skill-testing question administered by mail.

10. Simon & Schuster shall have no liability for any injury, loss, or damage of any kind, arising out of participation in this sweepstakes or the acceptance or use of a prize.

11. The winner's first name and home state or province will be posted on www.SimonSaysKids.com or the names of the winners may be obtained by sending a separate, stamped, self-addressed envelope to: Winner's List "Countdown Sweepstakes", Simon & Schuster Children's Marketing Department, 1230 Avenue of the Americas, New York, NY 10020.

Sarah.   Josh.

   Ariel.   Brian.

   Harold.   Julia.

         George.

Don't grow too attached to them.
They won't live long.